# SHERLOCK HOLMES

## vs.

## Jack the Ripper

***also by Frank J. Morlock***
Sherlock Holmes: The Grand Horizontals
***adapted by Frank J. Morlock***
Lord Ruthven the Vampire
*(adapted from Charles Nodier and Eugène Scribe)*
The Return of Lord Ruthven
*(adapted from Alexandre Dumas)*
Lord Ruthven Begins
*(adapted from Jules Dornay)*
Arsène Lupin vs. Sherlock Holmes: The Stage Play
(*adapted from Victor Darlay & Henry de Gorsse*)
Chéri-Bibi
*(adapted from Alevy & Marcel Nadaud)*
Frankenstein Meets the Hunchback of Notre-Dame
(*adapted from Charles Nodier,*
*Antoine Nicolas Béraud & Jean Toussaint Merle*
*and Victor Hugo, Paul Foucher & Paul Meurice*)
Gentlemen of the Night - Captain Phantom
(*adapted from Paul Féval*)
Nick Carter vs. Fantômas
(*adapted from Alexandre Bisson & Guillaume Livet*)
Rocambole
(*adapted from Auguste Anicet-Bourgeois and Lucien Dabril*)
Sherlock Holmes vs. Fantômas
*(adapted from Pierre de Wattyne & Yorril Walter)*

# SHERLOCK HOLMES

## vs.

## Jack the Ripper

Stories translated and adapted by
Frank J. Morlock

A Black Coat Press Book

Visit our website at www.blackcoatpress.com

ISBN 978-1-61227-038-8. First Printing. October 2011. Published by Black Coat Press, an imprint of Hollywood Comics.com, LLC, P.O. Box 17270, Encino, CA 91416.  Printed in the United States of America.

# TABLE OF CONTENTS

# *Introduction*

Jack the Ripper is one of the most enduring archetypes in criminal fiction. Over the years, the character has not only faced Sherlock Holmes, but a variety of other adversaries, ranging from Marvel Comics' *Eternals* to *Star Trek*'s Captain Kirk.

This book presents, for the first time in English, two of the earliest pieces of Ripper fiction ever written in French.

Gaston Marot & Louis Péricaud's stage play *Jack l'Éventreur* [*Jack the Ripper*] (1889) is probably *the* earliest French fictional work featuring the Jack the Ripper. Considering when it was written, one might say that it was torn from the day's headlines. The original play did not feature Sherlock Holmes and Nick Carter, but identifiable facsimiles thereof, for an audience that was already familiar with the Great English Detective and his indomitable American counterpart.

As earlier volumes of pastiches published by Black Coat Press have shown,[1] it was not unusual for French and German authors and publishers to imitate shamelessly such popular characters as Holmes, Dracula, etc. We have taken the liberty of using here the "real" names of such characters, as opposed to those used in the original

[1] See *Harry Dickson, Nick Carter vs. Fantômas* and *Sherlock Holmes vs. Fantômas*.

text: "Inspector Stevens" (Lestrade) and "Peter Weld" (Nick Carter).

The series of pulp magazines which later became *Harry Dickson* began in Germany in January 1907 under the title of *Detektiv Sherlock Holmes und Seine Weltberühmten Abenteuer* [*Sherlock Holmes and His Most Famous Cases*].

Published by Verlagshaus für Volksliteratur und Kunst, also responsible for Texas Jack (a Buffalo Bill imitation, 1906) and, later, Lord Lister (a Raffles imitation, 1908), *Detektiv Sherlock Holmes* was likely written by Theo von Blankensee and Kurt Matull, the creator of Lord Lister. It ran for 230 weekly issues, ending in March 1911.

The fact that the name of "Sherlock Holmes" was used on the cover created some concern about the possible wrath of Sir Arthur Conan Doyle's lawyers, so, with No. 11, the series was retitled *Aus den Geheimakten des Weltdetektivs* [*The Secret Files of the King of Detectives*], even though, inside, the main character was still called Sherlock Holmes. Doctor Watson, however, was soon replaced by a younger and more dynamic sidekick named Harry Taxon.

Sixteen issues of the original German series were adapted into French, between October 1907 and March 1908, by publisher Fernand Laven under the title *Les Dossiers Secrets de Sherlock Holmes* [*The Secret Files of Sherlock Holmes*]. That title appeared only on issue No. 1 and was immediately changed to *Les Dossiers Secrets du Roi des Détectives* [*The Secret Files of the King of Detectives*] with No. 2. Even though the hero was still identified as Sherlock Holmes.

One of the stories, *Wie Jack, der Aufschlitzer, gefasst wurde* (1908), No. 18 in the original German edition, No. 16 in the French edition, pit Holmes against Jack the Ripper. This was the first Holmesian pastiche in which the Great Detective matched his wits against Jack the Ripper.

Fans of pre-WWI Jack the Ripper fiction should also take notice of the seven issues published in 1909-10 in the *Sâr Dubnotal* series by Editions A. Eichler, Paris, who already put out Nick Carter, Buffalo Bill, Nat Pinkerton, Lord Lister and many other pulp series:
1. *Le Manoir Hanté de Creh'h-ar-Vran* [*The Haunted Manor of Creh'h-ar-Vran*]
7. *Tserpchikopf, le Sanglant Hypnotiseur* [*Tserpchikopf, the Bloody Hypnotist*]
8. *La Piste Astrale* [*The Astral Trail*]
9. *L'Écartelée de Montmartre* [*The Quartered Woman of Montmartre*]
10. *Jack l'Éventreur* [*Jack the Ripper*]
11. *Haine Posthume* [*Posthumous Hatred*]
Surely the most convoluted Ripper pastiche of all times, they formed a complicated saga in which Sâr Dubnotal, the Great Psychagogue, a mystic do-gooder trained in India, fought Tserpchikopf, an evil hypnotist and criminal mastermind, who was revealed to be Jack the Ripper. The series was translated (except for #8) by Brian Stableford and published by Black Coat Press as *Sâr Dubnotal vs. Jack the Ripper*, ISBN 978-1-934543-94-8.

In 1909, prolific pulp writer Arnoud Galopin, the creator of *Doctor Omega*, using the pseudonym of "Max Dearly," created a short-lived series of pulp magazines featuring young detective Allan Dickson, dubbed the "the Australian Sherlock Holmes" (which may well have been the inspiration for the name "Harry Dickson"). In one of these, Allan teamed up with his mentor, "Herlok-holms," to track down Jack the Ripper. Three years later, Galopin, who, like many other pulp authors of the times, liked to recycle his work, did a "patch-up" and combined two Allan Dickson stories, the one with Jack the Ripper and another, featuring a murderous, intelligent ape, and produced a novel, *L'Homme au complet gris* [*The Man in Grey*].[2]

Finally, in 1912, Jean Petithuguenin, a prolific science fiction author, penned *Jack l'Éventreur, le tueur de femmes* [*Jack the Ripper, Woman Killer*] as No. 3 in the series *Une aventure d'Ethel King, le Nick Carter fe-minin* [*An Adventure of Ethel King, The Female Nick Carter*], also published by Eichler. The *Ethel King* series lasted 100 issues, against 20 for *Sâr Dubnotal*. In that story, Jack was a serial killer who traveled from America to London to continue his murderous spree—and kill Ethel King.

Jean-Marc Lofficier

---

[2] Scheduled to be translated and published by Black Coat Press.

# JACK THE RIPPER
# (1889)

*Stage Play by*
*Gaston Marot & Louis Pericaud*

## CHARACTERS

INSPECTOR LESTRADE
NICK CARTER
CONSTABLE STONE
CONSTABLE TRENT
A SERGEANT
FIRST DETECTIVE
SECOND DETECTIVE
KITTY, a.k.a. THE LITTLE VIRGIN
BETTY BLACKTHORN, a.k.a. BETTY PATTERSON and VICTORIA TREVOR
MR. ROBINSON
SIR WILLIAM HUXELL
SIR JAMES PLACK
MISS ELLEN PLACK
BROOK
MASTER TONY
TOPPS
BARTLETT
RICKFORD

MERSON
A DRUNKEN WOMAN
TOM BROWN a.k.a. LORD MAXWELL
TOBY
MARY CLARWICK
COLLEEN, a.k.a. THE IRISH GIRL
A BUTLER
A NEWSBOY
ANOTHER SERGEANT
ELIZABETH JACKSON
JANE GOODMAN
ANNA WILKINS

Detectives, Soldiers, Men, Women, etc.

The action takes place in London in the 1880s.

# *ACT I*

## *SCENE I*

The office of Inspector Lestrade of the London Police. There is a door at the back, and two side doors. In the back, there is a telephone to the right of the Inspector's desk. To the left, facing him, the desk of the Constable. Armchairs, chairs.

AT RISE, Stone is at his desk to the left. Six detectives are standing before him.

STONE: I warn you that Inspector Lestrade is very unhappy with your performance. London is chockfull of criminals. You know their hideouts, their habits, their descriptions, and yet, you let them steal, rob and murder! Ah, truly, honorable gentlemen, one would almost think that you had an understanding with them. (*protests*) Yes, yes, I know! You're incapable of such things! Nonetheless, I warn you, if in three days, you haven't discovered the author of the recent crime in Piccadilly, you will be mercilessly kicked out of the London Police. They'll reassign you to the suburbs! You hear, gentlemen, to the suburbs! Now, you may leave!

(*The detectives bow and leave by the left. Trent enters from the right, papers in hand.*)

TRENT: Mr. Stone?

STONE (*rising*): Mr. Trent.

TRENT: Have you filed the Manning file?

STONE: Yes, Mr. Trent, by order of Inspector Lestrade.

TRENT: Fine. What about the nocturnal attacks?

STONE: They continue, despite the fact we've hung eight bandits so far. In my opinion, you see, Mr. Trent, their leader, the leader of the band, still remains to be caught.

TRENT: You believe that, Mr. Stone?

STONE: I would swear to it, Mr. Trent. It's a marvelously built organization, that one, to rival the Gentlemen of the Night of fifty years ago. Their attacks are planned with an audacity to which we're not accustomed. Inspector Lestrade himself can't quite believe it. And what is even more irritating for our national pride is that we're expecting this very day the visit of Nick Carter, the famous American Detective who's coming to pay tribute to the admirable workings of our police force.

TRENT: What will he say seeing that crimes are still unpunished and so many criminals yet to be apprehended?

STONE: Don't mention it! I am humiliated, confused, crushed with shame. England's honor is at stake!.

(*Inspector Lestrade enters from the back, preceded by a Sergeant who opens the door from him.*)

LESTRADE: Yes, gentlemen, and as we all know, England is the first nation in the world. (*The two Constables bow*) What news, today, gentlemen?

TRENT: Very little, Inspector... (*reading from the papers he holds*) Three break-ins in Regent Street, an attempted poisoning in Oxford Street, and a man crushed by a cab in the Strand.

LESTRADE: An Englishman?

TRENT: French.

LESTRADE: Ah. Keep going.

TRENT (*continuing*): Thirty two women publicly intoxicated, four infanticides…

LESTRADE: Fine! Fine! (*to Stone*) What about you?

STONE (*reading from his papers*): A brawl between two women of the Salvation Army. Two wounded men, grievously, a third man fell, stone dead, 942 persons of all sexes and nations robbed of their wallets in Hyde Park. Three hanged men in Limehouse...

LESTRADE (*excitedly*): Englishmen?

STONE: No. An Irishman, a Scotsman, and a Chinese.

LESTRADE (*calmly*): Continue.

STONE (*continuing*): An attempted derailment on the Woolritch line, seventeen houses robbed, fourteen deaths by imprudence….

LESTRADE (*heading to his desk*): Fine! Fine! Nothing much, indeed. London is becoming the quietest city in the world.

SERGEANT (*appearing* ): Mr. Nick Carter, the American Detective, solicits the honor of being received.

LESTRADE (*to the Constables*): Go, gentlemen.

(*Trent and Stone bow and leave*.)

LESTRADE (*to the Sergeant*) Show him in.

(*The Sergeant introduces Nick Carter and leave*.)

LESTRADE (*standing up, at his desk*): How do you do, Mr. Carter.

NICK CARTER: How do you do, Inspector.

LESTRADE: Please have a seat.

NICK CARTER (*sitting to face Lestrade*): Thank you.

LESTRADE (*sitting also*): I believed you arrived yesterday?

NICK CARTER: Yes, I did.

LESTRADE: You had a good trip, I hope?

NICK CARTER: Quite nice, thank you.

LESTRADE: This is the first time I've had the honor of meeting you. Please allow me to shake your hand. (*rising*)

NICK CARTER (*also rising*): Gladly. The honor is all mine.(*they shake hands and sit down*) Pardon me, Inspector Lestrade, for abusing your time…

LESTRADE: I'm only too happy to be at the service of a friendly ally.

NICK CARTER: Friendly—from time to time.

LESTRADE: We will surely reach a point where it will always be so.

NICK CARTER: I desire the same thing.

LESTRADE: So, you're here to…?

NICK CARTER: To study the workings of the London Police. Our men are as good as yours, but we have fewer successes. We have many villains who escape our justice. Here, almost all criminals pay their debts to society. Why? What are your procedures that enable you to arrive at such success?

LESTRADE: My dear Mr. Carter, there's a French axiom that says, "Find the woman." I've changed that to

"Unleash the woman." And through that tactic, I succeed every time.

NICK CARTER: I confess I don't understand.

LESTRADE: It's easy. I've inducted into my service the fifty prettiest women in London, organized in squads, like my detectives, and placed by me into all strata of society, from the mud of Whitechapel to the salons of Saint James. These women belong to me. I hold them all in my hand, ready to crush those who might betray me! No one knows their identities except me. Thus, I do not fear indiscretion. They are my things. I mould them to my will. A grand and majestic lady before whom a prince might bow is, in reality, nothing but my slave. I hold her by adultery, because she is married and I know her lover. A word from me and she is ruined; and her lover, too. So she has no choice but do my bidding. Another woman who might wallow in the hovels of the city, or was fished out of the Thames yesterday, is also my creature. I promised her gold, which she loves. I give her as much of it as she wants and through her, I know all the secrets of the bandits and the killers whose mistress she is, when I order her to become so.

NICK CARTER: I see! Very clever!

LESTRADE: Thank you. At this moment, London has fallen prey to a gang of villains who murder and pillage, even in the most frequented thoroughfares. A month ago, I sent twelve of my women on the trail and, through them, eight bandits have already fallen into my power.

NICK CARTER: Eight?

LESTRADE: With a single blow.

NICK CARTER: These women had become the mistresses of these villains?

LESTRADE: Yes. It was a certain Lucy Elliott who denounced her man Thompson to me.

NICK CARTER (*rising*): Ah!

LESTRADE: That interests you?

NICK CARTER: Deeply!

LESTRADE (*coming out from behind his desk*): I hold this girl through fear, on account of a crime to which I knew she was an accomplice. I offered her a choice between 20 years of hard labor or a reward of 50 pounds. She didn't hesitate long, and Thompson was quickly arrested, tried, condemned, and hanged. Another one, Mary Clarwick, whom I knew lusted for money, gave up her lover, Merwin, to me for a consideration of 25 pounds. Merwin met the same fate as Thompson.

NICK CARTER: So, all these wretches were given up, sold, by their mistresses?

LESTRADE: Yes, all of them! I haven't yet got the whole gang yet; the head is what I want. But I'll have him, I swear that to you!

NICK CARTER: That's marvelous.

SERGEANT (*entering*): Sir! The Little Virgin's here.

LESTRADE: Ah?

SERGEANT: They've arrested her for fighting with a drunken old woman.

LESTRADE: Fine. Show her in.

(*The Sergeant leaves.*)

NICK CARTER: The Little Virgin? Who's she?

LESTRADE: A girl from the streets whose marvelous beauty and shy manners got her that nickname. But in reality, her name is Kitty.

NICK CARTER: Kitty?

LESTRADE: She's the mistress of one of our most formidable thieves whose cleverness is only matched by his boldness. He's the one whom I suspect of being the head of that gang I was telling you about just now. And it's through her that I will take him down.

NICK CARTER: Through her? How fascinating…

VOICE OF BETTY BLACKTHORN: I tell you, I'll strangle her rather than leave her here with you!

LESTRADE (*to Nick Carter*): Keep to the side.

(*He goes to his desk. Nick Carter sits in a corner at the left, takes a newspaper, and pretends to read. Two detec-*

*tives enter, pushing Betty Blackthorn, a ragged old woman, before them.*)

BETTY BLACKTHORN (*howling*): Bring her in! Bring her in, too! I've found her! I won't let her go!

(*Then Kitty enters, escorted by two more detectives, and goes to the left.*)

NICK CARTER (*at the back, aside*): It's her!

LESTRADE (*to Betty*): I know you.

BETTY BLACKTHORN: That's possible.

LESTRADE: What did you do this time to be brought up before me?

BETTY BLACKTHORN: Nothing at all! Your detectives have got it in for me. They're swine.

FIRST DETECTIVE: She's a termagant.

BETTY BLACKTHORN: Me, a termagant? I'm the very lamb of God!

SECOND DETECTIVE: She was beating this young girl and wanted to drag her away. We arrested her and we brought her to you, Sir.

LESTRADE: What is it you call yourself now?

BETTY BLACKTHORN: Betty Blackthorn.

LESTRADE: The last time, it was (*thinking*) Betty Patterson.

BETTY BLACKTHORN: The name of the chap who loved me then.

LESTRADE: What do you do?

BETTY BLACKTHORN: I raise chickens.

LESTRADE: And where do you live?

BETTY BLACKTHORN: A bit further under the bridges than before.

LESTRADE: Are you still always drunk?

BETTY BLACKTHORN: I have the right! I joined two temperance societies!

LESTRADE: You're not the mother of this young girl?

BETTY BLACKTHORN: Me, her mother? I'd rather have my tongue pulled out! Does she even have a mother?

LESTRADE: Why did you assault her

BETTY BLACKTHORN: To teach her obedience.

LESTRADE (*to the detectives*): Keep her in custody.

(*The detectives grab Betty.*)

BETTY BLACKTHORN (*struggling*): Don't you touch me!

SECOND DETECTIVE: Come on! And shut up!

(*They push her toward the door.*)

LESTRADE (*to Kitty*): Come forward, child.

(*Kitty comes forward.*)

LESTRADE: Do you know that woman?

KITTY: To my misfortune.

BETTY BLACKTHORN: What's she saying, the little minx… (*making an attempt to get at Kitty*)

FIRST DETECTIVE (*holding her*): Will you be silent!

LESTRADE (*to Kitty*): Explain yourself.

KITTY: This woman abused me when I was a child.

BETTY BLACKTHORN (*foaming*): Oh! If only I get hold of you!

KITTY: I don't intend for her to abuse me as a young woman.

BETTY BLACKTHORN (*going to the desk*): Your Honor, I bought her when she was little! Bought and paid! She belongs to me!

KITTY: I've broken that chain! I'm free! I don't owe her anything anymore! I don't want to see her!

BETTY BLACKTHORN (*struggling*): Then let me claw her eyes out!

(*The detectives hold her back.*)

LESTRADE (*to the detectives*) Take her away!

BETTY BLACKTHORN: You're arresting me? You have no right!

SECOND DETECTIVE: Let's go! March!

BETTY BLACKTHORN: No! You'll have to carry me! You'll have drag me away! I won't walk!

(*Lestrade gives a sign.*)

FIRST DETECTIVE: Come on, on your way!

(*The detectives drag Betty away despite her howls.*)

LESTRADE (*to Kitty*): Fear nothing, child. You are under our protection. That woman said you were purchased?

KITTY: Or stolen.

LESTRADE: What about your parents?

KITTY: I never knew them. Betty had me in her possession as a child, the wretch! I remember all the bad treatment she inflicted on me, all the blows she gave me.

LESTRADE (*looking at her*): Like that scar I see there on your face.

KITTY (*with a sad smile*): Oh, that, sir. That's a souvenir from my childhood... (*resuming*) Betty wanted to sell me to some gentleman, and because I repulsed him, she beat me bloody. She deprived me of bread and water, and sent me to shiver on a dung heap. So I decided to end it. That was six months ago. I wandered the streets, begging. At first, what I received from the generosity of passers-by provided for all my needs. But then, I felt exhausted, my limbs aching, a circle of fire pressed on my face, my hands burning, my throat dry. I suffered! An intense fever seized me. I fell, almost choking in the street. What happened? I don't know, but when I opened my eyes, I was stretched on a bed. A man was near me, watching over me and caring for me...

LESTRADE (*rising, going to her*): What happened then?

KITTY: I never left him.

LESTRADE: So you became his mistress?

KITTY (*lowering her head*): Yes.

LESTRADE: How old are you?

KITTY: I must be 18 or 19.

LESTRADE: You love that man who sheltered you?

KITTY: Yes.

LESTRADE: What's his name? (*silence*) You're not answering? I asked you for his name.

KITTY: I don't know it.

LESTRADE: That's hardly credible. What does he do?

KITTY: I know nothing about that.

LESTRADE: You don't live with a man for six months without knowing who he is or what he does.

KITTY: And yet I don't.

LESTRADE: In that case, tell me what you do know.

KITTY: To me, he's good and generous; he loves me and I love him; that's all there's to tell.

LESTRADE: But when you question him, when you chat with him, what do you call him?

KITTY: I call him my friend.

LESTRADE: It's his name I'm after. What is it?

KITTY: I told you, I don't know.

LESTRADE: Fine. Where does he live?

KITTY: Everywhere and nowhere.

LESTRADE: It's obvious you don't wish to talk.

KITTY: I have nothing to tell you on his account. About me, you can have whatever you like.

LESTRADE: Beware, Kitty…

KITTY: Of what? I committed no crime; a woman, a wretch, wanted to hit me. Your officers came and took us both away, that's all.

LESTRADE: I have the right to lock you up.

KITTY: I know.

LESTRADE: But I don't wish to. You're free to go!

KITTY: Thank you, sir.

LESTRADE (*returning to his desk*): I'm still interested in you. When you find yourself in some sort of fix, come to me and I'll protect you.

KITTY: I won't forget.

(*She bows and leaves.*)

NICK CARTER (*rising*): What a strange girl.

LESTRADE (*running to his telephone*): Hello. Are Mary Clarwick and the Irish Girl still here? (*listens and replies*) Great! Let the Irish Girl follow Kitty, the one nicknamed the Little Virgin, who just left my office. Have her stay on her trail until she learns the name of her lover. As for Mary, she must, by tomorrow, no later, deliver to me the secret of the person she mentioned to me earlier. It's urgent!

NICK CARTER: Inspector Lestrade, I admire you.

LESTRADE (*returning to his desk*): Thank you. Within 24 hours, I will have learned everything I want to know.

NICK CARTER: Accept my compliments. But who is that Irish Girl who's detailed to follow the Little Virgin?

LESTRADE: A superb creature. She's the one who helped us arrest Cross, the famous strangler.

NICK CARTER: Ah!

LESTRADE: As for the person whom Mary Clarwick mentioned to me earlier… (*thinking better of it*) No, I can't tell you anything yet… But Mary is clever, skillful, pretty, and stops at nothing. She will become the mistress of that man and wrest his secret from him.

NICK CARTER: What about the old woman? The one who wanted to carry off the Little Virgin by force? What do you plan to do with her?

LESTRADE: Make her one of my auxiliaries who can render me some services in the future.

NICK CARTER: Yet, you're keeping her in custody…

LESTRADE: Only until tonight. This evening, I'll set her to watch Kitty.

NICK CARTER: She as well?

LESTRADE: Yes. She hates Kitty. She'll do a good job. After we have another conversation, I'll set her free.

SERGEANT (*entering*): A Mr. Robinson to see you, sir.

LESTRADE: Who's he?

SERGEANT: I don't know, but he claims to have information about the murder in Piccadilly.

LESTRADE: Show him in.

(*The Sergeant leaves.*)

NICK CARTER: The murder in Piccadilly?.

LESTRADE: A vulgar murder committed for theft, which has no real importance in proportion to the sum stolen. We haven't yet been able to discover the perpetrator. (*gesturing for Nick Carter to sit on the chair near his desk*)

(*Robinson enters; he is a portly man with a jolly, rubicund, somewhat naive face.*)

ROBINSON: Inspector Lestrade, I'm truly honored. (*seeing Nick Carter*) Oh, forgive me, you are not alone. In that case, sir, I have the honor of being your servant.

LESTRADE: You said you have information to give us about the murder in Piccadilly?

ROBINSON: Very important information, sir, very important indeed.

LESTRADE: Well, then, speak. What do you know?

ROBINSON: Am I to say everything? The name of the killer?

LESTRADE: Yes! His name, his age, his address, his habits and antecedents. (*ready to write*) I'm waiting.

ROBINSON: Excuse me, I beg you, would be so kind as to let me doze off. (*sitting down before the desk at the left*)

LESTRADE: Let you doze off? Why?

ROBINSON: In order to reveal the truth. Because, you see, sir, I am a sleepwalker.

LESTRADE: A sleepwalker?

ROBINSON: Yes, and when I am asleep, I speak. I see the truth. Note, sir, that I doze off easily and that I am of surprising lucidity.

NICK CARTER (*low to Lestrade*): He's a fool.

LESTRADE (*to Nick Carter*): I agree. (*to Robinson*) May I ask you what are your means of existence?

ROBINSON (*rising*): I'm a landlord. I own a house in Oxford street, one in Soho Square, and one in the Strand. I have 5000 pounds income.

NICK CARTER: Five thousand pounds?

ROBINSON: Yes, sir. (*sighing*) I've been married five times.

NICK CARTER: Five times?

ROBINSON: Yes, sir! And five times my wives have obtained a divorce because, at the moment of showing them I was not a somnambulist, I showed them exactly the opposite.

LESTRADE: You dozed off?

ROBINSON: Yes, sir! I've never really had any luck. I was run over three times by cabs. Because of that, I still bear a placard with me.

NICK CARTER: A placard?

ROBINSON: Here it is. (*producing a card from his pocket and reading*) "Good people who find me in the street, be kind enough to take me to my domicile in Redbourn Street. There will be a reward."

(*Carter writes Mr. Robinson's address on his sleeve.*)

ROBINSON (*continuing*): And note again, sirs, that I must be extra-lucid. I must unveil some astonishing truths, because each time such an accident happens to me, I never find my wallet in my pockets afterward.

NICK CARTER: And you believe that, in your sleep, you told the kind folks who found you wandering about: There's money in my wallet?

ROBINSON (*naively*): Well, yes. How could they know it otherwise?

NICK CARTER (*smiling*): That's true.

ROBINSON: Thus, I thought that this extraordinary case of somnambulism might be useful in protecting England, my country. And I've come to place myself at the disposal of the Metropolitan Police

LESTRADE: I don't believe greatly in the power of magnetism. Still, one must not disdain any help offered. I thank you for the urgency you've shown to assist justice. I will keep your name and your address on file.

ROBINSON (*sadly*): Then you don't want to watch me doze off?

LESTRADE: No, not right now. Later, perhaps. At the moment. I'm very busy.

SERGEANT (*entering*): I was given this card to deliver to you at once, sir.

LESTRADE (*taking the card and reading*): Sir William Huxell! By Jove! Is he in London? (*to the Sergeant*) Show him in!

(*The Sergeant leaves. Lestrade rises and ushers Robinson through the other door.*)

LESTRADE: Mr. Robinson, please leave this way.

ROBINSON (*radiant*): A private door, just for me? Ah, sir, you overwhelm me! Mark my words: I will be useful to you and to Great Britain. To serve one's country while asleep—that's no ordinary thing.

LESTRADE (*making him leave*): Indeed! Now go! Go!

ROBINSON: I'm going, I'm going. (*enthusiastically*) I am working with the police! What glory, what glory!

(*Robinson leaves.*)

NICK CARTER: It's difficult to believe that such fools exist.

LESTRADE: England is the leading country in the world when it comes to fools. We've got every kind of them.

NICK CARTER: I can go too, if you wish to be alone?

LESTRADE: No, stay put. I have nothing confidential to say to Sir William.

(*Nick Carter returns to his seat. Then, Sir William Huxell enters and goes to Lestrade. He is accompanied by a man and a woman.*)

SIR WILLIAM HUXELL: Inspector Lestrade, please allow me to shake your hand.

LESTRADE: With all my heart.

SIR WILLIAM HUXELL (*introducing the other two newcomers*): May I introduce Sir James Plack and his daughter, Miss Ellen Plack (*as an afterthought*) my fiancée.

SIR JAMES PLACK (*bowing*): Inspector Lestrade. (*greetings all around*)

SIR WILLIAM HUXELL: Sir James has a request to make of you.

LESTRADE (*going to James*): Speak, sir. What is it?

SIR JAMES PLACK: Not quite a request—rather, a service, an immense service which I am begging from you.

LESTRADE: A service?

SIR JAMES PLACK: So you can grasp the importance of it, it is necessary—indispensable—that I give you precise details.

LESTRADE: I'm listening to you, sir.

(*Lestrade goes back to sit behind his desk, Sir James follows him. The Sergeant brings up a chair for Ellen.*)

SIR JAMES PLACK (*pointing to Nick Carter*): Can I speak before this gentleman?

LESTRADE: You certainly can. This is Mr. Nick Carter, the famous American detective.

(*They exchange bows and take seats.*)

SIR JAMES PLACK: You know my name, Sir William just informed you of it. I've been married for 18 years, am the proud father of two children, two girls. The elder (*pointing to Ellen*) was barely three when I found myself in a shocking state of misery. (*reaction by Lestrade*) Oh, I have nothing to be ashamed of, because I'd done nothing to deserve it.

LESTRADE (*in a kindly manner*): Please continue, sir.

SIR JAMES PLACK: One night, when I came home, my wife, who hadn't eaten all day, proposed that we kill ourselves, together with the children.

LESTRADE: Oh!

SIR JAMES PLACK: I lacked the courage to see the children whom I adored die. An agency had just opened to enroll men to accompany an illustrious explorer who was going to attempt the exploration of the interior of Africa. They were offering a bonus to those who signed on. I rushed to this agency and I signed up, bringing to my wife and children, if not well being, but at least assuring them of a decent life for a little while longer. Then I left.

ELLEN PLACK: My poor father!

SIR JAMES PLACK: Yes, poor me. (*resuming*) We were to travel to lands unknown further than Senegal and Sudan. But a storm tossed us on the coast. There, a savage tribe ravaged our ship, destroyed it completely, and took us prisoners to the interior of the country. I saw all my companions perish one by one. For some reason, my life was spared. I lived for 15 years in the desert with that wandering tribe, far from any civilization. Eventually, their warlord died. Because I had rendered some services to these ignorant creatures, they proclaimed me their king. I didn't waste any time taking immense riches into my possession. Then I opened relations with the Europeans, and at long last, I succeeded in reclaiming my freedom and returning to England to bring wealth and happiness to my wife and children.

SIR WILLIAM HUXELL: I was the one who was lucky enough to free Sir James from his royal captivity.

SIR JAMES PLACK: When I arrived in London, I discovered that my poor wife had dead for a long while. A sister of hers had brought up my little Ellen. As for my other daughter, who had been entrusted to the care of a wet-nurse, she had disappeared.

LESTRADE: Disappeared?

SIR JAMES PLACK: That miserable woman had left the poor little thing with an orphanage because we had been a few months late paying her. That, at least, is what she told my wife's sister, when, sometime later, she came to fetch the child. Indignant, my sister-in-law rushed to the orphanage, but there, they claimed that on the day indicated by the nurse, they had received no child. It was all a lie. My sister-in-law informed the police who planned to make the wretched woman tell the truth, but she hurriedly disappeared and we've never heard of her since.

LESTRADE: That does indeed presents lots of difficulties.

ELLEN PLACK (*rising*): I'm certain you will overcome them, sir, for my father's happiness, and mine.

LESTRADE: I will do all that it is in my power to do. (*to Sir James*) Where do you live, sir?

SIR JAMES PLACK: Belgravia.

(*Nick Carter writes the address in his notebook.*)

LESTRADE (*also writing*): Thank you.

SIR JAMES PLACK: When I returned, my first care was to seek out those who were everything to me. In this task, too, Sir William seconds me like a son.

SIR WILLIAM HUXELL: Shouldn't I, sir?

SIR JAMES PLACK: It's thanks to him that I've rediscovered my wife's sister, and Ellen. But Clary, my poor Clary, what's become of her? (*Two o'clock strikes.*)

NICK CARTER (*rising*): Two o'clock. Pardon me, but I'm obliged to leave you.

LESTRADE: We will see each other again soon surely?

NICK CARTER: It's very nice of you to say so, Inspector, for I'm indeed counting on troubling you further.

LESTRADE: You will never trouble me.

NICK CARTER (*smiling*): We shall see. (*pointing to the door by which Robinson left*) Where does this door go?

LESTRADE: Whitehall.

NICK CARTER: Can I use it, without committing an indiscretion?

LESTRADE (*accompanying him*): Of course, you can.

NICK CARTER: (*as he passes Sir James, Sir William and Ellen*) Gentlemen… Miss Ellen… (*all bow*) Inspector… (*shaking Lestrade's hand*) Thanks.

(*Nick Carter leaves by the door indicated.*)

SIR WILLIAM HUXELL (*to Lestrade*): I ought to tell you, Inspector Lestrade, that I saw this Nick Carter jot down Sir James' address just as you were doing so.

LESTRADE: Uh-oh! Might he like to best me in that investigation and discover something before I do?

SIR WILLIAM HUXELL: Why would he want to do that?

SIR JAMES PLACK: Yes. To what end?

LESTRADE (*going to his desk*): To humiliate England by solving the case before I do!

(*There is a sudden uproar of voices in the antechamber; the Sergeant appears.*)

LESTRADE (*leaving his desk*): What's going on now?

SERGEANT: A man—no, make that a lunatic—pretending to be the famous American Detective Nick Carter insists on seeing you.

LESTRADE (*to himself*): How can that be? What does this mean? (to Sir James, Sir William and Miss Ellen) Would you like to leave this way? (*he indicates the door on the left*) I shall be in touch very soon.

SIR JAMES PLACK: Thank you, Inspector!

(*They leave.*)

LESTRADE: Show that man in.

(*The Sergeant leaves and returns with a man who absolutely looks like the Nick Carter who was just there.*)

NICK CARTER (*agitated*): Is it to Inspector Lestrade that I have the honor of speaking?

LESTRADE: Yes.

NICK CARTER: Inspector Lestrade, I am Nick Carter. I disembarked yesterday in London. Two men were waiting for me on the dock, saying they were sent by you. I followed them without suspicion. They got me into a carriage and, once inside, threw themselves upon me, blindfolded me and took me—where? I don't know. At our destination, two other men garroted me, gagged me and carried me to a cellar where they left me, saying, "Fear nothing, we know who you are. Tomorrow at 2 o'clock, you will be free." Today, when 2 p.m. struck, I was brutally escorted, with the same precautions, to within a quarter of a mile of my hotel. Here are my papers, my passport, all the documents necessary to convince you that I am whom I claim to be. (*gives them to Lestrade*)

LESTRADE (*hastily examining them*): By Jove! Yes! You *are* Nick Carter! But then, who was the other man? (*suddenly*) Ah, Mr. Carter, we have both been tricked by an audacious bandit! A man presented himself here in your place, under your name. He even had borrowed your facial features.

NICK CARTER: But to what purpose?

LESTRADE: I don't know.

(*Constable Trent enters.*)

TRENT: An urgent letter, sir.

LESTRADE (*taking the letter and opening it*): Who brought it?

TRENT: An errand boy.

LESTRADE (*reading*): "Dear Inspector Lestrade: By this time, you probably know that I mystified you. I needed to find out how you were so successful in arresting my companions. You had the kindness to explain your methods and identify your associates. I thank you greatly for that. Those who betrayed us, who caused my comrades to be hanged, will die despite anything you and all the detectives in England might do. Kindly receive, Inspector Lestrade, my sincerest salutations. I'm all right. Signed: Jack."

NICK CARTER: Jack?

LESTRADE: It's a challenge! Very well, I accept it! We shall see who will win the game.

CURTAIN

## *ACT II*

### *SCENE II*

A tavern in a narrow alley by Bishop's Gate. There is a door at the back, and doors to the right and left. In the middle of the stage, a little to the right, there is a usable trap door. There is a counter in the back at the left. Behind it, there is a window with curtains of red cotton. A few candles light this sleazy and smoke-filled lair. There are tables to the left and right, and chairs.

AT RISE, two sinister-looking men, dressed in hideous rags, but all wearing top hats, are sitting at one of the tables with several women. They are listening to Master Tony, the executioner, who, standing on a chair, is holding court. Brook, the landlord of this hovel, goes to the table chatting and serving his customers.

VOICES (*drunken and hoarse*): Hey, Brook! Some gin! Brandy! Port! (*all bang the table*)

BROOK: Coming! Coming!

TONY: Look here. Are you going to listen to me, yes or no?

ALL: Yes, yes! Speak!

BROOK (*serving*): A conference on the art of hanging given by the executioner of London in person. One should always listened to that.

TOPPS (*seated at a table*): But that doesn't prevent us from drinking.

BROOK: I should hope not!

TOPPS: Speak, speak, Master Tony!

ALL: Yes, yes!

TONY: Honorable gentlemen, I've chosen the tavern of the esteemed Mr. Brook as being one of the most ill-famed of the neighborhood of Bishop's Gate… (*general grumbling*) No use grumbling, it's well known by everyone. Even the most honest of you, ladies and gentlemen, deserve to have passed through my hands at least ten times. (*all laugh*) You laugh; I prefer that! That's because, one day or another, sooner or later, you will be hanged. Therefore, I conceived, with humanitarian intent, the notion of edifying you about what some misguided souls have dubbed, and still refer to, as the extreme penalty…

TOPPS: Hell! It seems to me that it is rather extreme…

TONY: Poppycock! It's a pleasure!

TOPPS: To get oneself hanged?

TONY: If I say it's so, it's so. I know more about it than anyone else in England. What the Hell! You won't suffer, my lads, after I've placed a fine collar of real hemp around your neck and I've launched you mercifully into space. First of all (*all listen with curiosity*), a bright light will dazzle you. Then, goddesses will appear, dancing all around you. You will mingle with them and you will pass away without sorrow, without pain, dreaming of *la vie en rose* and the Mohammedans' paradise.

ALL: Hurrah! Hurrah!

TONY: So hold back your tears when you finally come to me. No rage. No sudden ideas that might prevent me from doing my job well. Let me hang you gently, like the brave thieves and carefree murderers that you are, and trust in my experience, which will send you deftly into the next world!

ALL: Hip, hip, hurray! Hip, hip, hurray! Long live Master Tony! Long live the hangman of London!

TONY: Thank you, my friends, thank you! Now a last glass of gin to my health and good night.

BROOK (*giving him a glass*): You're leaving us?

TONY: Yes. I promised your colleague Dietrich in Whitechapel a small talk, similar to yours, and it's getting late. I don't want to risk myself in your neighborhood after ten in the evening.

TOPPS: Would you like us to escort you?

ALL: Yes, yes!

TONY: Thanks, my friends, thanks. Here goes to my health, honorable and ladies. (*he drinks*)

ALL: To Master Toby's health!

TONY: And to the pleasure of not seeing you again, except in the exercise of my functions.

ALL: Long live Master Tony!

(*Tony and a group of cutthroats leave* )

TOPPS: That executioner is really a nice chap.

BROOK: And he has more guineas in his strong box than I have hair on my head.

TOPPS: What was the purpose of this talk he gave us?

BROOK: I've heard there's a question in high circles of replacing the gallows with the French Guillotine.

ALL: No! No! Never!

BROOK: And Master Tony has a horror of blood. Rather than consenting to guillotine a man, he will hand in his resignation, much as he loves his job.

TOPPS: He's right. Long live the gallows!

ALL: Yes, yes! Hurrah for the gallows!

(*Bartlett enters, followed by his companions Rickford and Merson.*)

BARTLETT: Plague! It's merry in here!

TOPPS: Ah! Bartlett! So?

BARTLETT: So it's done. At 2 o'clock precisely, the American was put out the door.

RICKFORD: With all the care that was due him.

MERSON: If the boss had listened to me, the bloke in question would never again have seen the fogs of London

BARTLETT: Bah! What do have we to fear from him?

MERSON: You never can tell. The living talk, the dead never do.

BARTLETT: What could he say, even if he had the notion to speak? We blindfolded him, took him to the house in Euston Square, locked him in the coal cellar, and at the hour indicated by the boss, we put him back on the pavement, his eyes still blindfolded. He didn't see us, he doesn't know us. Complete security.

BROOK: Who's this man you're talking about?

RICKFORD: We'll tell you about him when we're alone.

BARTLETT: Hey, companions, now's the time for us to separate.

DRUNKEN WOMEN (*seated*): Already?

TOPPS: Haven't you had enough, dearie?

DRUNKEN WOMAN: Never enough.

RICKFORD (*to the others*): Take her away. Until to-morrow.

ALL: 'Till tomorrow!

(*They leave, dragging off the drunken woman.*)

BARTLETT: Nine o'clock! Will the boss come?

(*Tom Brown enters, dressed as a worker.*)

TOM BROWN: He has come.

ALL: Tom Brown!

TOM BROWN: Hey! I'm thirsty. Brook, some wine!

BROOK: Coming! Coming!

TOM BROWN (*looking around*): No one here who shouldn't be here?

BARTLETT: We are alone.

TOM BROWN: That's fine. (*to Brook who brings a glass and a bottle*) What's this?

BROOK: The Port you asked me for.

TOM BROWN: Am I in the habit of drinking alone? Glasses for everyone, and another pint.

ALL (*going to sit at the table*): Hurrah!

TOM BROWN (*sitting, facing them*): I want you to drink with me. Drink to vengeance.

ALL: To vengeance!

TOM BROWN: Yes! Listen to me. And let my words be graven in your minds! Eight of our companions have been hanged.

ALL (*somberly*): Alas!

TOM BROWN: Do you know who gave them up?

ALL: No!

TOPPS: Do *you* know?

TOM BROWN: By God, I do now. They were given up by their mistresses.

ALL: Ah!

TOM BROWN (*rising, and coming forward, followed by his gang*): Yes, by their mistresses, who were paid by the police to spy on them and sell them out.

ALL: Ah!

TOM BROWN: It was to discover this that I had you kidnap Nick Carter, the American from New York. By impersonating him at Scotland Yard, I knew they would reveal to me their methods of ferreting us out.

BARTLETT: Will these wretched women remain unpunished?

TOM BROWN: Unpunished? Ah, you cannot think that! I am going to exact a terrible oath from you. You are going to swear to serve me blindly in the vengeance I am going to undertake.

ALL: Speak!

TOM BROWN: Those who betrayed us, be they sisters, even mothers, of one of us, will be mutilated, disemboweled, cast on the public way, as a challenge to society, and as a challenge to the police. No voices will be raised asking mercy for her.

ALL: We do swear it!

BARTLETT: The names of these women?

TOM BROWN: You know them: Mary Clarwick, Elizabeth Jackson, Mary-Ann Nichols, Annie Chapman, Elizabeth Stride, Catherine Eddowes, and Mary Jane Kelly.

ALL: They will all die!

TOM BROWN: That's well. And from now on, beware of your mistresses!

BARTLETT (*following Tom Brown to the bar*): Kill all the women, I say!

ALL: Yes! Kill all the women!

TOBY (*head emerging from the trapdoor*): Kill all the women? How ya gonna do it?

ALL: Toby!

TOBY: I beg your pardon for having come through the tunnel, but I thought the street door would be locked at this time.

(*He emerges from the trapdoor, then shuts it.*)

BROOK: You did well, kid.

TOBY: Ah, don't kill all the women. Leave some of them alone. I'm only 16 and I haven't had time to try them out. Let me get to know 'em first, then kill 'em afterwards.

TOM BROWN: Shut up, kid, and come here.

TOBY: Coming, boss.

TOM BROWN: Did you succeed?

TOBY: Easily! I presented myself to the person in question. He asked me who I was. I said I was a man whose magnetic power can revive the dead, while throwing some fluid into his face. (*making a comic gesture*) He looked at me with his big, stupid eyes and asked if I was trying to put him to sleep. I said, yeah, but I want you to imagine, in your sleep, that you are awake. And so on and so forth. More fluid! Then, he says he feels he's asleep, but not asleep.

BARTLETT: Now there's an idiot.

TOM BROWN: Shut up! (*to Toby*) Continue.

TOBY: Then I said to him that Inspector Lestrade wanted him to come around 10 p.m. to this tavern, and I told him how to get here.

TOM BROWN (*excited, walking around*): And he'll come?

TOBY: Twice rather than once.

TOM BROWN: Great! And at his place?

TOBY: Just an old sewing woman and some furniture. That'll make you want to have what he has. (*goes to speak to Brook*)

TOM BROWN: We will have it. (*to the others*) At midnight, at 38 Redbourn Street, the home of Mr. Robinson.

ALL: Fine!

TOM BROWN: Only an old woman servant. Put her to sleep with chloroform, and steal the gold, banknotes and jewelry. You'll find me at the entrance to Clark Street in two hours.

BARTLETT: Understood.

TOM BROWN (*to Toby, who comes forward*): You, you know what you have to do.

TOBY: Keep that man here as long as possible.

TOM BROWN: At least until new orders. (*pause*) And now, my friends, I'm expecting someone...

TOBY: The pretty Miss Kitty. I bet a pound I'm not mistaken

TOM BROWN: You win. You owe yourself a pound. Remember, the dear little thing is unaware who I am.

BROOK (*leaving his counter*): Didn't you convince her you were an Irish conspirator?

TOM BROWN: Yes. Now, not a word that might betray me.

BROOK: Say there, boss. If she denounces you to the police after the oath we just took, we'll have to treat her like all the others.

TOM BROWN: Her? Yes, sadly, it would be necessary. But we'd die together, because if I kill her, I'd be killing myself.

(*Knocking at the back.*)

BROOK: Oh, oh. Let's put out the lights. (*puts out candles*) Who can that be?

TOM BROWN: It cannot be Kitty. I told her to meet me here at 11 p.m.. (*to Brook, pointing to the trapdoor.*) The boys are there?

TOBY: Yes. I saw them coming.

TOM BROWN: That's fine. (*low to Brook*) Answer this way: "I only open to the police."

BROOK (*going to the back*): I only open to the police.

MARY CLARWICK (*outside*): It's me, Mary! Open up!

TOM BROWN: Mary Clarwick! Merwin's mistress.

RICKFORD: Yes, it's she! I recognize her voice.

MARY CLARWICK (*outside*): Well! Will you open up?

TOM BROWN (*to Brook*): Open!

(*Brook opens the door; Mary enters.*)

MARY CLARWICK: How dark it is in your place, Mr. Brook.

TOM BROWN: You love the light, Mary, well, here's some.

MARY CLARWICK: Tom Brown. Ah, it's you I was searching for.

TOM BROWN: To make you forget Merwin?

MARY CLARWICK: Perhaps! Regrets are not eternal. I love him even now, the poor lad. The cowards hanged him. The hangman, Mr. Tony, gave me a piece of the rope. Here it is. It will bring me luck!

TOBY: Give me a bit of it, Mary.

MARY CLARWICK: No! The rope that hanged a man you loved, that's sacred.

TOM BROWN: More sacred than the life of the one you loved, right, Mary?

MARY CLARWICK: The way you say that to me... Do you doubt the affection that I had for Merwin?

BARTLETT (*to her right, mockingly*): A bit.

TOPPS (*to her left*): A lot!

MERSON, RICKFORD, AND TWO OTHER MEN: Passionately!

TOBY (*going to Mary*): Oh, not at all!

MARY CLARWICK: And you, Tom Brown, you're not answering me. Why?

TOM BROWN: Mary, how much did Inspector Lestrade give you for denouncing your lover?

MARY CLARWICK: What are you talking about?

TOM BROWN: How much did he promise you to denounce me in my turn, if you got to be my mistress and revealed my secrets to you?

MARY CLARWICK: Are you mad?

TOM BROWN: Mad! You'll see! My friends (*all rise*) this girl was adored by our poor friend Merwin. He stole to buy jewels for her. It was for her that he murdered a banker in Manchester! Well, as thanks for all that, this wretch sold him to Scotland Yard. This girl deserves to die.

ALL: Yes! Yes!

MARY CLARWICK: You're mistaken! I swear to you that you're mistaken. I didn't denounce Merwin! I didn't sell out my lover!

TOM BROWN: Do you know who told me?

MARY CLARWICK: Who was it? Tell me his name so I can spit in his face.

TOM BROWN: Inspector Lestrade himself!

MARY CLARWICK (*forgetting herself*): Ah, the coward! He betrayed me!

TOM BROWN: As you've just betrayed yourself. Come on! Take her away!

MARY CLARWICK: Help! Help!

(*One of the men gags her as the others tie her up.*)

TOBY (*opening the trap door*): The coal cellar is open.

(*Two men drag Mary down.*)

TOM BROWN (*deadly*): I'll be back.

(*He takes a knife from the table and follows them.*)

TOBY: Christ! I wouldn't want to be in her skin.

BROOK: Me neither! The Boss can be ferocious when he puts his mind to it.

(*knocking.*)

TOBY: That must be my man!

BROOK (*at the door*): Who's there?

ROBINSON (*outside*): Me! Mr. Robinson!

IRISH GIRL: And me!

BROOK (*low*): He's not alone!

IRISH GIRL: Open without fear; we are friends.

BROOK (*opening*): Enter Milord and Milady!

ROBINSON: Is this really the tavern of the honorable Mr. Brook of Bishopsgate?

BROOK: The honorable? Why, that's me.

IRISH GIRL (*to Brown*): You see, Mister, I didn't deceive you. I know the reputation of Mr. Brook's pub.

ROBINSON: Thank you, Miss.

BROOK (*aside*): I recognize her. She's the Irish Girl.

TOBY (*to Bartlett, Rickford, & Topps*): Go!

BARTLETT: Right.

(*They leave quietly.*)

ROBINSON: Mr. Brook, I am Mr. Robinson.

TOBY (*coming forward*): And you've come to see me, right?

ROBINSON: Ah, yes. It's him! It's him. (*to himself*) My magnetizer!

IRISH GIRL (*aside*): No one except this innkeeper, the old idiot, and this boy.

ROBINSON (*to Toby*): Well, young man, you told me to come and I came. What can I do for you?

TOBY: You can… But excuse me, this lady is with you…

IRISH GIRL: I don't know this gentleman. I just helped him to get here, that's all.

TOBY: In that case, it would be really nice if you were to… You know… (*gestures for her to leave.*)

IRISH GIRL: To leave? That's no big thing. There's nothing here but Mr. Brook's tavern.

ROBINSON (*aside*): What? She's leaving?

IRISH GIRL (*aside, at the door*): The Little Virgin isn't here! I've lost her track. But I'll find it again. (*aloud*) Good night.

(*She leaves.*)

ROBINSON (*to Toby*): Excuse me, but…

TOBY (explosively): Mr. Robinson! (*spewing fluid on him*)

ROBINSON (*stumbling*): A commotion!

TOBY (*continuing*): Inspector Lestrade asked you to come here to undertake a confidential mission with me.

ROBINSON: A confidential mission? Speak, speak, young man!

TOBY: No need to tell you that I am part of it, right?

ROBINSON: It's apparent right away from your honest face. What is it about?

TOBY: This: Bandits are going to come here…

ROBINSON: Here?

TOBY: Yes.

ROBINSON: The Devil!

TOBY: They're coming here to plot and scheme.

ROBINSON: A plot? Well! They won't succeed! What plot?

TOBY: It's about robbing an honest citizen who had the imprudence to leave his home.

ROBINSON: People are such fools!

TOBY: Oh, yes.

ROBINSON: Such a thing would never happen to me. Ah, no indeed.

TOBY: You're too smart.

ROBINSON: I am especially lucid!

TOBY: Well, if the bandits have their plan, Inspector Lestrade has his, too.

ROBINSON: That makes two plans. That of Inspector Lestrade must be more honest than that of the bandits! I associate myself with his plan heart and soul! What must I do?

TOBY (*pointing to a door*): Go in there.

ROBINSON: In there?

(*Toby pretends to spew some fluid on him.*)

ROBINSON: I will! I will! That's fine!

TOBY: And try to overhear the conversation of the bandits.

ROBINSON: And—what about you?

TOBY: Me? I'll be hiding over here. (*pointing* ) I'll listen, too.

ROBINSON: I get it. And putting together what we both hear, we'll have it all, complete, homogenous and incontestable.

TOBY: There you go!

ROBINSON: It's gigantic!

TOBY: What a man! What a man!

ROBINSON (*modestly*): That's simply because I'm a genius.

TOBY: Oh, yes. Quite modest too. Come on. Let's go!

ROBINSON: Oh, the love of intrigue! The love of intrigue!

(*He leaves.*)

TOBY (*locking the door after him with a key*): And now, old chap, listen all you like. If you hear a word of what's going to be said here, I'll buy you a sandwich, and a glass of pale ale!

BROOK: Ah, indeed! What are you planning to do with that fine, fat chap?

TOBY: Nothing. In two hours, you'll set him free.

BROOK: And what shall I tell him?

TOBY: That the plan failed.

BROOK: Right.

(*Eleven o'clock can be heard striking. Tom Brown returns. He locks the door after him, and controls his emotions.*)

TOM BROWN Eleven o'clock!

TOBY (*to Brook*): The Boss!

TOM BROWN (*to himself*): Kitty should be here soon.

(*Knocking at the back.*)

TOM BROWN: Not a word. You don't know me. (*going to sit down*)

(*Kitty enters.*)

KITTY: Mr. Tom Brown, if you please.

BROOK: He's here! Come in, Miss.

(*Brook locks the door and goes to his counter*)

TOM BROWN (*rising and going to Kitty*): Kitty!

KITTY: You told me to come at eleven, it's eleven, and here I am!

TOM BROWN: Right, Kitty, my pretty darling! (*kisses her*)

KITTY: Oh. Not in front of everybody!

TOM BROWN (*laughing*): Everybody, indeed! An innkeeper, and a drunken apprentice who are not paying attention to us.

KITTY:(*sitting at the table*): When is this going to end? When are we going to be able to see each other in broad daylight?

TOM BROWN (*sitting down beside her*): Soon, perhaps! When will Ireland be free? Denounced, hunted down, I had to flee to escape the condemnation pronounced against me! But don't be alarmed! Good times will come again—even if they are slow to come. We'll go away, leave England! You don't want to stay in London, do you?

KITTY: I want to stay with you, forever! Near you, the one I love!

TOM BROWN: But what if you were to find your parents?

KITTY (*rising*): Parents? Only lucky people have parents.

TOM BROWN: Maybe you're meant to see them again one day, who knows?

KITTY: I've often said that to myself.

TOM BROWN (*rising*): Ah?

KITTY: Yes. Then I started to dream I was in my mother's arms, my father's too. My imagination gave them faces. I wonder if they are but distant memories. Are they omens? I don't know. But it seems to me that one day, all this will happen.

TOM BROWN: And if it does happen, and you became rich, would you still love me?

KITTY: I would become your wife. You saved me from death; I owe you my life!

TOM BROWN: My beloved darling! (*they kiss for a long time*)

KITTY: But are these mad, crazy ideas?

TOM BROWN: Who knows? Maybe it will happen.

KITTY: Ah, you don't know who I am. I don't want you to talk about it.

TOM BROWN: No, no! Only I have faith in the future, and I'm waiting, with you…

KITTY: I'm really afraid that we've waited too long. Listen, I was arrested today.

TOM BROWN (*feigning surprise*): You?

KITTY: Yes. For having resisted that wretched old woman I've told you about.

TOM BROWN: Betty Blackthorn?

KITTY: Yes. That evil woman found me again, pursued me and tried to drag me away by force. Then two policemen came and took us to Scotland Yard.

TOM BROWN: And?

KITTY: Inspector Lestrade himself questioned me about you! He tried to get me to talk. To give you up! But I didn't say anything! However, he knows that I love you. He even tried to make me into a spy, and I'm afraid.

TOM BROWN: Don't worry. My precautions are taken, and well taken! I have nothing to fear.

KITTY (*placing her hands on his shoulders and looking at him*): Ah, Tom Brown, if you would just…

TOM BROWN: Just what?

KITTY: Tell me everything, all that you are thinking, all that worries you, all that threatens you…

TOM BROWN: Why, you know, my pretty little thing, I'm hiding nothing from you. Soon, I will be completely yours, all yours.

KITTY: Are you telling me the truth?

TOM BROWN (*embarrassed*): Yes! Yes! But for now, return to your lodgings.

KITTY: Aren't you coming with me?

TOM BROWN: No! But I probably will join you soon. Go! 'Till later.

(*As Brook opens the door to let Kitty leave, Betty Blackthorn enters like a fury.*)

BETTY BLACKTHORN (*knocking over a chair and rushing to the bar*): Something to drink!

KITTY (*frightened, she rushes to Tom Brown*): Betty! She followed me!

BLACKTHORN: Drink, I said!

KITTY (*low*): She's drunk!

TOBY (*laughing*): Like a skunk!

BETTY BLACKTHORN (*leaving the bar*): Ah, is there anyone here?

BROOK (*behind the bar*): There's me.

TOBY (*going toward her*): And me, venerable crone!

BETTY BLACKTHORN: That's all? Ah, no… I spy a little snout of a woman in that dim corner… With her lover, no doubt. Ah, ah! Love! Isn't it nice! It has rough thorns that tear right to the blood. (*taking a glass from the counter and drinking*) Why, it's nice all the same. I knew love once.

TOBY: Under Cromwell!

BETTY BLACKTHORN (*taking a few drunken steps, lurching toward Toby*): What's he saying?

TOM BROWN (*low, to Kitty*): Get out of here.

(*He goes to the door with her.*)

KITTY: 'Till soon.

(*She vanishes.*)

BETTY BLACKTHORN: The little girl left. I love youth. I'm going to follow her.

TOM BROWN (*stepping in front of the door, which he locks*) No you won't!

BETTY BLACKTHORN: Huh?

TOM BROWN: Do you know me, Betty Blackthorn?

BETTY BLACKTHORN (*leaning on him*): Heavens! You know my name?

TOM BROWN: Yes.

BETTY BLACKTHORN: No, I don't know you, but I didn't say anything bad about you. I want to leave now.

TOM BROWN (*grabbing her arm and pushing her*): No, you're not leaving.

BETTY BLACKTHORN (*falling into a chair*): Why not? What do you want from me?

TOM BROWN (*very near her*): I've heard you've been working for the police…

BETTY BLACKTHORN: Me?

TOM BROWN: Yes, you. Your job is to follow Kitty, so as to discover the identity and address of her lover, about whom Inspector Lestrade has suspicions.

BETTY BLACKTHORN (laughing hideously): Ah, ah, ah, ah! (*she stops as abruptly as she began*) How mistaken you are, sir! I'm interested in that child only because I'm her mother. I brought her up, and she runs away from me, the ingrate little bitch, and I am going to find her, so she can provide for me for the remainder of my poor old age. That's all. (*rising, and imperiously drunk*) So let me follow her, and be quick about it.

TOM BROWN: I said: No!

BETTY BLACKTHORN (*losing patience, trying to get by him*): Lemme go!

TOBY (*aside*): Hmm. I think she's not drunk anymore.

TOM BROWN: Listen to me, and don't try to argue with me. You're wasting my time and time is money. We're birds of a feather you and I, aren't we? But you don't know me, while I have the advantage over you, since I know who you are.

BETTY BLACKTHORN: Lemme go!

TOM BROWN: I don't think so. This isn't your lucky day. First, Inspector Lestrade, and now me. In truth, I doubt very much you'll be rendering the Police any useful services... (*taking her arm*) I've got you now, and I won't let you go.

BETTY BLACKTHORN (*trembling, looking at him in the eyes*): You… (*a pause, as she stares at him*) You won't kill me?

TOM BROWN (*eyes riveted on hers*): Why shouldn't I?

BETTY BLACKTHORN: Then you are…?

TOM BROWN: Yes.

BETTY BLACKTHORN (*getting away from him and screaming*) Ah, Mercy! (*she falls on her knees*)

TOM BROWN: You are confessing then?

BETTY BLACKTHORN: Yes! Yes! But I swear I'll keep my mouth shut! I swear it!

TOM BROWN: I don't trust you, Betty Blackthorn, but you may still save your skin...

BETTY BLACKTHORN (*rising*): I ask nothing more. What must I do? Speak, and I will obey.

TOM BROWN: You must be honest.

BETTY BLACKTHORN: Oh, as for me, honesty…

TOM BROWN: And tell me the truth about this young girl you claim you've raised.

BETTY BLACKTHORN: What do you want to know?

TOM BROWN: Do you know her real family?

BETTY BLACKTHORN: No, as sure as you are a man and I'm a woman, I do not.

TOM BROWN: How old was Kitty when she fell into your hands?

BETTY BLACKTHORN: Two years old.

TOM BROWN: How did you get her?

BETTY BLACKTHORN: I stole her.

TOM BROWN: You're lying.

BETTY BLACKTHORN: By all the Saints in Heaven, I swear to you I'm not! She was playing in Hyde Park with other little girls. She wore earrings and I carried her off for her poor little jewels, not for her… Anyway, I was embarrassed by it afterwards. I wanted to throw her in the Thames. (*Tom Brown reacts angrily*) Hell! She could ruin me. But I've got a good heart, so I brought her up! Now that's the truth, the whole truth.

TOM BROWN: And you didn't seek to discover who her parents were?

BETTY BLACKTHORN: What for?

TOM BROWN: That's fine. And that's enough of that!

BETTY BLACKTHORN: I'm free. I've saved my life?

TOM BROWN: Saved your life, yes. Free, no. (*calling*) Brook!

BROOK (*leaving the bar*): What's up?

TOM BROWN: Open the boudoir.

BROOK: Right. (*opens the trap door*)

BETTY BLACKTHORN (*terrified*): You promised me!

TOM BROWN: If you told the truth! You lied to me! Until you tell me the truth, I'm going to put you in a safe place.

BETTY BLACKTHORN: I swear to you I told you the truth!

TOBY (*grabbing her roughly*): Don't swear, old woman! It's as if you were singing!

TOM BROWN (*grabbing her in his turn and pulling her toward the trapdoor*): Are you down there, the rest of you?

VOICES (*from below*): Yes!

TOM BROWN: Catch this package!

BETTY BLACKTHORN: No! No! I will talk! I will talk! Help me! Help me! Help! Help!

(*With Toby's help, for Betty resists with the valor of terror, Tom Brown hurls her into the cellar.*)

BETTY BLACKTHORN (*screaming*): Aaaaah!

(*She vanishes and Brook calmly shuts the trapdoor. At this moment, the sound of a police patrol is heard. The noise travels from right to left and becomes distant. Brook quickly blows out the candles, then remains motionless as do Toby and Tom Brown. All listen attentively.*)

BROOK: A police patrol.

TOM BROWN (*standing on the trapdoor*) They're going away.

TOBY (*neck extended*): We'll be at peace now for another two hours!

(*A ray of moonlight filters through the window, piercing the red curtains, lugubriously lighting the stage. Tom Brown gestures to Toby and Brook. Toby heads towards the door at the left, opens it and gives a hand signal. Brook goes to the door at the back, opens it, and inspects the street. Two men enter from the back carrying the bloody cadaver of Mary Clarwick. They enter slowly, preceded by Toby who leads them. They pass by Tom Brown who points to the door at the back, and they leave.*)

TOM BROWN (*stopping in the doorway*): That's how all those who've betrayed us will die!

(*He leaves. Brook leaves behind him.*)

CURTAIN

## *SCENE III.*

A dark, hideous street in Whitechapel, a sort of square. To the left, there is a hovel whose interior is visible. In the hovel, there is an old mattress, a table and a chair.

(*Toby enters, followed by the two men bearing the cadaver of Mary Clarwick. Toby lights the way for them and is alert.*)

TOBY No one. (*to the two men*) Come on, the rest of you.

(*The men walk in slowly and vanish, still following Toby. After they've disappeared, Nick Carter appears following them. Then Carter vanishes too. Tom Brown emerges from the fog.*)

TOM BROWN (*stopping suddenly before the hovel*): Ah, Kitty's dwelling. Let's make sure of a refuge in case of pursuit. (*he takes a key and opens the door, then listens*) Somebody! (*looking*) A woman? A spy, perhaps? No, it's Kitty! Let's not let her see me.

(*He disappears following Toby and the two men. Kitty enters.*)

KITTY (*pensive*): To go away! To leave England! Yes! But where else could we live happily? Still, it must be done. I've convinced him to do it, and we'll expatriate ourselves as soon as possible.

(*The Irish Girl enters from the right.*)

IRISH GIRL *(to herself)*: Yes, it's she! It's really she! (*she hides*)

KITTY: What he said to me troubles me. Why did he talk to me of my parents? Why did he want to revive hope in my heart? My parents? No. I will never know them. Ever!

(*She heads towards the hovel.*)

IRISH GIRL (*aside*): That's where he has his refuge, our Mr. Tom Brown!

KITTY: Heavens! My door is open! Has Tom Brown come?

(*She goes into the hovel and lights a candle. Meanwhile, the Irish Girl comes forward and explores the surroundings, then disappears. Kitty lights her lodging and looks about.*)

KITTY: No one! Perhaps, I forgot to latch it. (*she sits near the window in a chair by the door.*) Ah, if those who abandon children knew the sorrows they cause them, the tears they bring, the tortures they inflict on the poor beings that God sent to them, instead of casting them on the pavement, exposing them to chance on the high roads, if they would clasp them in their arms, pull them to their breasts and suffocate them instead, with a last caress! Death would be better! A kindness compared to the wretched existence to which the abandoned are condemned! I no longer have parents! I am alone in the world. (*she extinguishes her light and stretches out on her mattress*)

(*The Irish Girl comes to the door and tries to look inside.*)

IRISH GIRL: I'd like to go inside.

KITTY: May God forgive them, as I forgive them despite all the wrongs I have suffered.

(*She dozes off; two o'clock strikes in the distance.*)

IRISH GIRL: Oh, well, the evening has been good! Inspector Lestrade will be pleased. I know where the woman lives; they will watch over you now, Little Virgin, and if you are part of the gang, so much the worse for you. (*noise on the right*) Someone!

(*She squats down near the hovel. Bartlett and Rickford enter from the right.*)

BARTLETT: Do you see him?

RICKFORD: No!

(*Merson and Topps enter behind them.*)

MERSON: He can't be late! He told us two o'clock, and two just struck!

TOPPS (*looking to the left rear*): Ah!

BARTLETT: It's him?

TOPPS: Yes.

(*Tom Brown returns with Toby.*)

TOM BROWN: So?

BARTLETT: Good business! Jewels, bank notes and gold. (*giving it all to Tom Brown*)

TOM BROWN: Excellent. You've written all that down?

RICKFORD: Oh, the inventory was carefully made. (*giving Tom Brown a paper*) Here's the account. You can check it.

TOBY: There's got to be order in business!

TOM BROWN: We'll divide the loot tomorrow.

BARTLETT: What about Mary Clarwick's corpse?

TOM BROWN: Placed at the corner of Cleveland Street, with a knife in her belly and a ribbon in her hair.

TOBY: And the knife is beautiful and carefully signed.

TOM BROWN: Now, let's split so as not to awaken any suspicion.

ALL: 'Till tomorrow.

(*They all leave in different directions.*)

TOM BROWN: I must absolutely get into the home of this James Plack, his millions tempt me. (*thoughtfully*) But the means? (*pause*) I think I've found them!

(*He walks towards the hovel.*)

IRISH GIRL (*standing up*): Who's that man going into the Little Virgin's house?

TOM BROWN (*stopping abruptly*): There's someone here!

(*With a leap, he hurls himself at the Irish Girl, seizing her by the throat.*)

IRISH GIRL: Help! Help!

(*Tom Brown drags the Irish Girl to the right.*)

TOM BROWN: Ah! Will you shut up!

IRISH GIRL (*in a strangled voice*): Don't hurt me! I'll shut up!

TOM BROWN (*clasping her throat*): Who are you?

IRISH GIRL: Why do you want to know?

TOM BROWN: Who are you? Answer me!

IRISH GIRL: They call me the Irish Girl.

TOM BROWN (*exploding*): The Irish Girl!

IRISH GIRL (*screaming*): Help!

KITTY (*waking up*): Huh? What?

(*She stands up and goes to the door.*)

TOM BROWN: You gave up Cross! You've been condemned. You will die!

(*Tom Brown wrestles the Irish Girl to the ground. At that moment, Kitty opens the door, comes out and stands in the doorway.*)

KITTY: What's going on?

(*She comes out of the hovel.*)

IRISH GIRL (*screaming*): Help! Help!

TOM BROWN (*raising his knife*): Here!

(*Tom Brown stabs the Irish Girl. At this moment, a ray of moonlight illuminates the scene, enabling Kitty to recognize him. He, however, has not realized that he is being watched.*)

KITTY: Ah! Him! Him!

(*Tom Brown savagely stabs the Irish Girl, who dies.*)

TOM BROWN: And now go tell Lestrade how Jack the Ripper avenges himself!

(*He leaves quickly by the right.*)

KITTY (*recoiling with horror*): Ah!

(*Nick Carter emerges from the shadows and follows Tom Brown.*)

CURTAIN

## *ACT III*

### *SCENE IV*

Belgravia Cottage. To the left, there is an elegant residence with a double flight of stone steps. To the right, mid-stage, a rustic pavilion of modest appearance. There is a grilled gate at the back, with a large door in the middle. Next to the door, on the left, there is a bench. There are two large trees to the right and left of the gate, and some garden furniture.

AT RISE, James Plack, William Huxell, and Ellen Plack are seated at a table on the left taking tea.

SIR WILLIAM HUXELL: No news yet from Inspector Lestrade?

SIR JAMES PLACK (*holding a paper which he's been perusing*): No, and that makes me uneasy. Inspector Lestrade promised to inform me as soon as he was on a trail having some credibility. Here we are, three days later, and still nothing!

ELLEN PLACK: A little patience, father. London is huge.

SIR JAMES PLACK: Yes. (*reading his paper*) Yet another murder committed last night in Whitechapel.

SIR WILLIAM HUXELL: A new murder?

ELLEN PLACK: Another poor woman?

SIR JAMES PLACK: Yes! This makes three! Who is the monster that goes after these poor wretches so furiously?

SIR WILLIAM HUXELL: A madman, doubtless.

SIR JAMES PLACK: This time, again, as in the last three days the killer has warned the Police and signed his letter "Jack the Ripper."

ELLEN PLACK: Father, don't read that.

SIR JAMES PLACK: You're right. (*after a pause*) You asked, Sir William, why I've chosen this neighborhood of London to purchase this home?

SIR WILLIAM HUXELL: I confess to seeing in this decision only a millionaire's caprice.

SIR JAMES PLACK: Leave my millions out of it. By installing myself in this house I wanted, if God lets me find the child I'm weeping for, to help her memory.

SIR WILLIAM HUXELL: So it was here that you lived when you decided to tempt fortune in Africa?

SIR JAMES PLACK: Yes. (*pointing to the pavilion*) Over there! Since then, they've built this house. (*pointing to the elegant house*). Everything has been furnished with the greatest luxury, but I've insisted that they respect the pavilion, this garden, these huge trees, in the end, everything that is still capable  of striking the imagination of my poor little Clary, when, as a baby, she ran and played in these beautiful walks.

SIR WILLIAM HUXELL: I understand. If, as must be hoped, we find her, they may awaken her memories.

SIR JAMES PLACK: Yes! (*to Ellen*) Ellen, what are you thinking of, my darling?

ELLEN PLACK (*rising*): About Clary! About my poor sister. I was very young when she was taken from us. I was hardly a year older than she was and yet it seems to me that I can still see her with her beautiful curly hair and her big blue eyes. Ah, Father, I want to see her again!

SIR JAMES PLACK: Dear child!

ELLEN PLACK: What's become of her? Maybe she's ill? She's weeping! She's calling us! She asks for me, too, and I loved her so much. Ah, Clary, Clary! Come back to us! Come back to us!

SIR JAMES PLACK: Let's hope, at least, that she is still alive!

ELLEN PLACK: Ah, father, don't talk like that! No, my intuition tells me my sisters still lives! I can feel it. If she were dead, that would be too frightful. God would not allow it.

(*A Butler appears on the steps.*)

BUTLER: Inspector Lestrade!

ALL: Ah!

SIR JAMES PLACK: Show him in as fast as you can!

(*The Butler disappears.*)

SIR WILLIAM HUXELL: For him to put himself out like this, he must have big news to tell you.

(*The Butler returns with Inspector Lestrade.*)

SIR JAMES PLACK (*going to him*): Inspector! Are you bringing joy to this sad home?

INSPECTOR LESTRADE: Perhaps.

ELLEN PLACK: My God!

SIR WILLIAM HUXELL: Ellen…

INSPECTOR LESTRADE: I need some information that you alone can give me which may speed things up.

SIR JAMES PLACK: Is it possible?

INSPECTOR LESTRADE: Oh, don't delude yourself with too much hope, because disappointment, if disappointment comes, would be too cruel.

SIR JAMES PLACK (*indicating the bench at the right and sitting beside him*): Question me, Inspector. I am ready to answer.

INSPECTOR LESTRADE: I believe I've found the nurse.

SIR JAMES PLACK: What are you telling me?

ELLEN PLACK: In that case, we are going to find out the truth!

INSPECTOR LESTRADE: Don't rush to hope too soon. You must understand that this woman has every interest in concealing the crime she committed. I am speaking only of the child confided to her care. For the moment, I do not wish to entertain the hypothesis of the child's death, but this woman is capable of anything.

ELLEN PLACK: My God!

INSPECTOR LESTRADE: In the last dragnet that I ordered…

SIR WILLIAM HUXELL: "Dragnet?"

INSPECTOR LESTRADE: It's an American term for which we have no equivalent and which reproduces quite exactly the action of sweeping everything in. But I digress. As I was saying, in our latest dragnet, we found a certain Betty Blackthorn, a monster, physically and morally, a combination of vulture and viper. Well, I'm of the opinion, I believe that Betty Blackthorn and the nurse—her name then was Victoria Trevor—are one and the same person.

SIR JAMES PLACK: Victoria Trevor… Yes, that rings a bell…

INSPECTOR LESTRADE (*rising*): Sir James, I need an exact description of the child that was stolen from you. Pardon for awakening such memories.

SIR JAMES PLACK (*sorrowfully*): My poor little Clary was a brunette.

INSPECTOR LESTRADE: Brunette.

ELLEN PLACK: With big blue eyes.

INSPECTOR LESTRADE: Blue eyes. What else? Did she have any particular marking that could specifically identify her, supposing we had someone in mind? That's what I must know.

SIR JAMES PLACK: I'm trying…

INSPECTOR LESTRADE: Think carefully, think hard.

ELLEN PLACK (*suddenly*): Ah! Hold on! Yes! Yes! I remember something! One day, in the garden, she fell and her face hit the root of a tree.

SIR JAMES PLACK: Yes, yes, I remember that too. It was just before I left.

ELLEN PLACK: She had a scar, here. (*she points to her face*) Right about here.

INSPECTOR LESTRADE (*shaking*): Ah!

SIR JAMES PLACK: What's wrong?

INSPECTOR LESTRADE (*controlling himself*): Nothing! (*aside*) Oh, that would be horrible.

ELLEN PLACK (*observing him*): My sister is still alive, right? And you know who she is?

INSPECTOR LESTRADE (*embarrassed*): Please, excuse me…

ELLEN PLACK: You're trembling! Pardon me if I insist on the truth—the truth rather than this dreadful doubt which is killing my poor father.

INSPECTOR LESTRADE: Control yourself, Miss Plack. As of yet, I am sure of nothing. I am still searching.

SIR WILLIAM HUXELL: Won't the word "hope" escape your mouth before you leave?

INSPECTOR LESTRADE: No. Hope is too strong a word at the moment.

ELLEN PLACK (*trying to read his thoughts*): Please!

INSPECTOR LESTRADE: Can we go into your office, Sir James? I have some questions that I want to put to you in privacy.

ELLEN PLACK (*with a scream of horror*): Ah! My sister is dead! And you don't want to tell me!

INSPECTOR LESTRADE: No, no! That's not the case at all. (*aside*) Better if she were, perhaps.

SIR JAMES PLACK: Come, Inspector.

INSPECTOR LESTRADE: Take courage, Miss, and trust in divine mercy.

(*He leaves with Sir James.*)

SIR WILLIAM HUXELL (*gently*): Ellen…

ELLEN PLACK (*collapsing onto the bench*): I am very unhappy, my friend.

SIR WILLIAM HUXELL: Ellen! You're tearing my heart apart.

ELLEN PLACK: Forgive me, my love! But knowing that I have a sister in this huge city, probably living in squalor… It chokes me like an iron collar, torturing me. And I am surprised I haven't gone mad yet!

SIR WILLIAM HUXELL: Ellen, calm down! Your feelings for Clary mustn't make you forget your love for your father.

ELLEN PLACK: My father!

SIR WILLIAM HUXELL: Think about him. Without you, he would die. You're everything to him; you are all he's got. Don't allow yourself to fall into despair. Give him courage and hope.

ELLEN PLACK: Yes, yes! You're right.

SIR WILLIAM HUXELL: You don't have the right to die, because your father needs you.

ELLEN PLACK: You are right, my friend. (*she grasps his hand tenderly*) I owe it to my father.

(Kitty, barely able to stand, appears at the gate and crouches by the bars)

KITTY: Help me! Help me!

(*She falls on the bench at the back. Sir William runs to her.*)

SIR WILLIAM HUXELL: A beggar girl!

(*Ellen runs to the table and pours some tea.*)

ELLEN PLACK: Why, she's dying!

(*She goes to Kitty, as William supports her*)

ELLEN PLACK: Here! here!

KITTY (*weakly, after having gulped down some tea*): I'm hungry.

ELLEN PLACK: Oh, the unfortunate woman! Help me, my friend, to get her to the table.

(*They support Kitty and lead her to the table*.)

KITTY: Thank you!

ELLEN PLACK: Here! Eat something!

SIR WILLIAM HUXELL: The poor child!

ELLEN PLACK: She's fainting from starvation.

VOICE OF A NEWSPAPER BOY: Another hideous murder in Whitechapel!

KITTY (*stops eating*): My God!

NEWSBOY: Horrible murder of two wimmin committed by (*screaming*) JACK THE RIPPER!!!

(*Kitty stands bolt upright*.)

ELLEN PLACK: What's the matter?

KITTY: Nothing! Nothing!

NEWSBOY (*appearing by the gate*): Bloodcurdling details! Description of the murderer! One pence.

KITTY: Ah! (*running to the boy*) Here, take it. Let me have it, let me have it!

NEWSBOY (*gives her the newspaper and goes away*): Hideous double murder in Whitechapel! (*his voice trails off to the left*)

SIR WILLIAM HUXELL (*watching Kitty*): All this excitement…

KITTY (*trying to read*): His description! Let's see, let's see! Ah, my eyes are clouded. I cannot see.

ELLEN PLACK: What's wrong with you, girl? What is it you want to know?

KITTY: The… the description of the murderer. There, there. I want to read it but I can't. Read it to me, please!

ELLEN (*reading*): "Jack the Ripper is a man of about fifty, built like a colossus, tall, broad-shouldered. His head and his beard are red. A reward of 500 pounds is promised to whoever gives him up."

KITTY (*breathing more easily*): Ah! (*she slowly takes back her paper and nods her thanks to Ellen*) (*aside*) They won't catch him! He's not the one they suspect. I still love him, but this is monstrous, infamous... What to do? What to do? (*she collapses on the bench.*)

SIR WILLIAM HUXELL: What can be wrong with her?

ELLEN PLACK: I don't know.

SIR WILLIAM HUXELL: So much emotion! Perhaps she knows the murderer?

ELLEN PLACK: What are you talking about? No, no! She's ill! She's weeping! (*going to Kitty*) Come to yourself, Miss. And takes some nourishment.

KITTY: You are kind, thank you!.

(*Supported by William, she comes to the table. Toby enters, dressed as a groom.*)

TOBY: A fine house. This is the place. It's a question of inspecting it by order of the Boss. (*coming forward*) Excuse me, milord and milady, I'm looking for the residence of a gentleman whose service I am to enter and I've lost his address. Lord Maxwell.

SIR WILLIAM HUXELL (*busy with Kitty*): He's not here, my lad.

TOBY: Sorry, milord. (*looking at the house, quickly and expertly*) The house door opens on the garden. Fine! (*bowing*) Milord, Milady. (*seeing Kitty, aside*) Her!

SIR WILLIAM HUXELL: Go, lad, go!

TOBY (*aside*): The Little Virgin! My Goodness! (*aloud*) Don't disturb yourselves, Sir, Madam. (*aside*) The Little Virgin here. What does it mean? Let's go find the boss.

(*He leaves.*)

ELLEN PLACK (*to William*): How beautiful she is!

SIR WILLIAM HUXELL: Yes! But what mystery hovers over this child?

KITTY (*rising, quietly*): You've helped me. Thanks you I'll never forget it! I'll be on my way now.

ELLEN PLACK: You are very weak.

KITTY: God will give me the strength.

ELLEN PLACK: Where are you going?

SIR WILLIAM HUXELL: You are without resources. You can't risk yourself like this on the road.

ELLEN PLACK: Let me come to your aid.

(*Ellen approaches Kitty and offers her money. Kitty takes it and suddenly breaks into sobs.*)

ELLEN PLACK: What's wrong with me suddenly? (*she shivers*)

SIR WILLIAM HUXELL (*supporting her*): Ellen!

KITTY (*to herself, slowly raising her head*): Ellen?

ELLEN PLACK (*to William*): It's nothing! It will pass off.

KITTY (*getting up and looking around for the first time*): My God! This place…

ELLEN PLACK (*to William*): See how moved she is!

SIR WILLIAM HUXELL: Yes… yes…

KITTY (*placing her hand over her face*): Oh, no, no! Am I am going mad? (*aloud*) Goodbye, Miss! Goodbye, Sir. Goodbye. (*she starts to leave, but staggers*) I can't! I can't!

SIR WILLIAM HUXELL (*supporting her, to Ellen*): It would be cruel to let her leave. (*pointing to the pavilion*) Miss, let's go there!

ELLEN PLACK (*to William*): Yes, you're right. She needs to rest a bit, a lot. (*to Kitty*) Come into the pavilion. No one will bother you, and when you feel stronger, you can go on your way.

KITTY: Ah, Miss, what have I done to deserve your kindness?

ELLEN PLACK: You are ill!

(*They lead her into the pavilion. Ellen and Kitty go in.*)

SIR WILLIAM HUXELL: What misery. And how many of these poor girls can one find on the streets of London?

(*Tom Brown enters, very elegantly dressed, followed by Toby, still dressed as a groom.*)

TOM BROWN: Sir James Plack, if you please.

SIR WILLIAM HUXELL: This is where he lives. He'll be with you any moment.

TOM BROWN: Thank you!

TOBY (*low*): Let's hurry. I'm getting cold feet as they say in America.

TOM BROWN (*to Toby, in a loud voice*): Mr. Bob?

TOBY: Milord?

TOM BROWN: Keep yourself at a respectful distance.

TOBY: Yes, milord. (*he goes toward the gate.*)

TOM BROWN (*aside*): I don't see her. (*to William*) Are you part of Sir James Plack's family?

SIR WILLIAM HUXELL: Almost, milord.

TOM BROWN: I understand! I understand! Sir James Plack, I am told, has a daughter, a charming person and she is promised to you, no doubt? (*William nods*) Allow me to present myself, Lord Maxwell of Liverpool.

SIR WILLIAM HUXELL: I know your name, milord, through your servant who barely an hour ago came looking for you.

TOM BROWN: For me? (*to Toby*) You were looking for me, Mr. Bob?

TOBY: I was looking for your lordship's residence.

TOM BROWN: You are very stupid, Mr. Bob.

TOBY (*feigning shame*):Yes, milord.

TOM BROWN (*to William*): To whom have I the favor of speaking?

SIR WILLIAM HUXELL: I am Sir William Huxell.

(*Sir James returns with Inspector Lestrade*.)

SIR JAMES PLACK: You have all the information that I could possibly provide you with, Inspector.

INSPECTOR LESTRADE: Thank you, Sir James!

TOM BROWN (*aside, seeing Lestrade*): Aie!

TOBY (*aside*): It stinks like cops here.

SIR WILLIAM HUXELL: Sir James, here's a gentleman who wishes to have a short conversation with you.

(*Sir James and Tom Brown bow to each other. Ellen comes out of the pavilion.*)

ELLEN (*to William*): She's resting now.

(*Both go to the door of the pavilion and look inside*.)

SIR JAMES PLACK (*to Tom Brown*): Sir?

TOM BROWN: Pardon me, Sir James, for coming to importune you. (*presenting himself*) I'm Lord Maxwell of Liverpool. I'm proposing to undertake an expedition into central Africa. I was informed that you had lived a long while there, and I came—forgive me again—to ask you for information which might be of the greatest use to me.

SIR JAMES PLACK: Excuse me, Milord, but I'm in the company of Inspector Lestrade of Scotland Yard, concerning a matter of the greatest personal importance.

TOM BROWN: Ah, this Gentleman is Inspector Lestrade?

INSPECTOR LESTRADE: I have that honor, sir.

TOM BROWN: Well, sir, I do not congratulate you with respect to the accomplishment of your duties.

INSPECTOR LESTRADE: Sir!

TOM BROWN: Never have so many crimes been committed, whose author you haven't even begun to discover. It's deplorable.

INSPECTOR LESTRADE: Sir!

TOM BROWN: Three unfortunate women were murdered in less than 48 hours in Whitechapel, without you and your men succeeding in arresting the wretch who revels in such atrocities, openly, in the heart of London. Go on, sir, admit that your police force utterly lack flair.

INSPECTOR LESTRADE (*furious*): Sir, I protest…

TOM BROWN: Pardon me!. We pay you and your men dearly enough to have the right to be discontent.

INSPECTOR LESTRADE: I will not allow you to speak to me in such a manner.

TOM BROWN: So be it! But in that case, protect me. Defend me. Defend my purse and my life. That is your job.

INSPECTOR LESTRADE: There are some circumstances, sir, before which all the resources available to the police are powerless.

TOM BROWN: These circumstances present themselves too often.

SIR JAMES PLACK (*to Tom Brown*): I beg you, Milord, to end a conversation that is too painful to me, seeing the great esteem that I have for Inspector Lestrade.

TOM BROWN: I obey you. I was wrong. I allowed myself to get carried away. I beg Inspector Lestrade to accept my humble apologies.

TOBY (*aside*): He pasted him with a solid right hand.

TOM BROWN: Still, all in all, we'd do better to employ Sherlock Holmes…

SIR JAMES PLACK: Please, Lord Maxwell.

(*Suddenly, Mr. Robinson rushes in from the rear, hat in one hand, kerchief in the other.*)

ROBINSON: Inspector Lestrade. Where is Inspector Lestrade? (*seeing them*) Pardon me. Apologies!

(*He collapses in a chair near the table.*)

TOM BROWN (*aside*): Robinson!

SIR JAMES PLACK: Who is this person?

INSPECTOR LESTRADE: A friend of the police. Will you allow me...?

SIR JAMES PLACK: Of course.

TOBY (*to Tom Brown, low*) You've gone very far, Boss. Let's get out of here.

TOM BROWN (*loudly, with confidence*): Mr. Bob?

TOBY: Milord?

TOM BROWN: Keep yourself at a respectful distance.

TOBY:(*aside*): Near the gate, yes. I much prefer that. (*aloud*) I'll wait outside, Milord.

TOM BROWN (*low*): No, keep looking for Kitty!

TOBY (*aside*): He's going to get us all nabbed.

(*Toby goes to the pavilion while Sir James confers with Tom Brown. Sir William and Ellen go to sit on the bench at the right.*)

INSPECTOR LESTRADE (*to Robinson*): What happened to you?

ROBINSON (*wiping his face dry with his kerchief*): Ah, Inspector, you are looking at a man who's been robbed!

INSPECTOR LESTRADE: Robbed? How?

ROBINSON: Yes, sir and it's my sleep that caused it. Damn sleep! If only I were not a somnambulist! But I don't want to be anymore. It's too costly!

INSPECTOR LESTRADE: Get to the point!

ROBINSON: Pardon me, pardon me. Allow me to catch my breath.

TOBY (*after looking inside the pavilion*): Ah!

(*He returns to Tom Brown.*)

ROBINSON: Thanks, now that I've caught my breath, I'll begin…

TOBY (*to Tom Brown, pointing discreetly to the pavilion*): She's in there.

TOM BROWN: Fine. What is she doing?

TOBY: She appears to be asleep.

ROBINSON: Here's the lamentable story. While I was locked in the dark in a tavern near Bishop's gate, on the mission on which you sent me, my house was ransacked.

INSPECTOR LESTRADE: A mission on which I sent you? Your house was ransacked.?

ROBINSON: Yes. As soon as I was released, I went home, with the intention of taking a nap in my nice feather bed. It's a luxury I indulge in, and my means permit it, or at least they used to. But now, I'm ruined.

INSPECTOR LESTRADE: Ruined?

ROBINSON: My houses remain, but all my cash, my valuables, the jewels of my five wives, all that was mine, has been stolen.

INSPECTOR LESTRADE: How much did they get?

ROBINSON: Around 20,000 pounds.

INSPECTOR LESTRADE: Now that's quite a sum!

ROBINSON: You can say that again! I'll say, it's a sum—an enormous sum.

INSPECTOR LESTRADE: And are you certain…?

ROBINSON: Am I certain? Unfortunately, yes, I am quite certain. I ran to your office, but they told me you were here. I walked. I no longer have a penny to my name to afford a cab. Ah, Inspector Lestrade, I beg you, please, get my money back.

TOBY (*aside*): I wouldn't count on that, old boy!

TOM BROWN (*to Lestrade*): Well, sir, what was I saying to you only a few minutes ago? (*to Robinson*) Allow me to shake your hand, sir. And to pity you with all my heart.

ROBINSON: Ah, you can't pity me more than I pity myself.

INSPECTOR LESTRADE We will consider the matter. You must return with me to Scotland Yard to make your complaint.

ROBINSON: But I just did; I made it to you.

INSPECTOR LESTRADE: That's insufficient and not according to procedure.

ROBINSON: You want tears?

INSPECTOR LESTRADE: There are certain formalities…

ROBINSON: Oh! Formalities! When will England be rid of them? (*he collapses into a chair*)

TOM BROWN: Decidedly, London is becoming uninhabitable. Sir James, I will have the honor of presenting myself to you another time. I'm in haste to leave this country. I shall feel safer among the savage populations of Africa. Please receive my greetings and my gratitude. (*bowing to Ellen*) Miss! (*to Lestrade*) Inspector, please recall the words of the great French philosopher: “A well constituted police force is the masterpiece of civilization.” I had the honor of meeting you. (*to Toby*) Mr. Bob?

TOBY: Milord?

TOM BROWN: Follow me!

(*They leave* )

INSPECTOR LESTRADE (*frostily, to himself*): Lord Maxwell of Liverpool. I will remember that name. (*to Sir James*) Whatever impertinent, ill-informed people may say, you may trust that we will spare nothing to protect the peace and tranquility of the subjects of Her Gracious Majesty.

SIR JAMES PLACK: I have no doubt of it, Inspector Lestrade.

INSPECTOR LESTRADE: Scotland Yard are the best police in the entire world. ’Till later, and you can count on me!

(*He shakes the hand of Sir James, who accompanies him to the gate. Then, Lestrade leaves.*)

ROBINSON: Pardon, I’m not leaving yet. I… (stu*mbling*) I feel… faint. I ran hard. I have bad legs.

SIR JAMES PLACK: Control yourself, man, control yourself!

ROBINSON: Thank you! You're very nice. Ah, by Jove! It's my cursed somnambulism. Now, it would be bad for me to simply doze off.

SIR JAMES PLACK: If you need to sleep, don't stand on ceremony, sir.

ROBINSON: You are really too kind! I am infinitely grateful to you. (*looking at the bench*) Ah, I notice a bench over there. May I stretch out?

SIR JAMES PLACK: Go ahead, sir, go ahead.

ROBINSON: Thank you again. The more emotional I am, the more sleepy I become. At the moment, I am asleep on my feet.

(*He goes to the bench and lies down.*)

ELLEN PLACK: Father?

SIR JAMES PLACK: What, darling?

ELLEN PLACK: Sir William and I have found a poor young girl.

SIR JAMES PLACK: A young girl?

SIR WILLIAM HUXELL: Who was dying of starvation and collapsed at our gate.

SIR JAMES PLACK: You did the right thing.

ELLEN PLACK: She couldn't continue on her way because of her weak condition, We put her in the pavilion where she's been resting.

SIR JAMES PLACK: We will see to it that she receives all necessary care.

ELLEN PLACK: Oh, father. How good you are!

SIR JAMES PLACK: Is merely coming to the assistance of those who are ill being good?

ELLEN PLACK: Father, my kind father. (*kissing and hugging him*)

SIR JAMES PLACK: Come, child, come Sir William. I am going to tell you what Inspector Lestrade told me, and what hope he has based on the descriptions that I gave him.

(*They go into the residence. Then, Kitty emerges from the pavilion.*)

KITTY (*gripped by a strong emotion*): At last! They're gone! I can look at this garden again, because I'm certain of it now. This is not the first time I've been here. Where did I see these huge trees before? Where did I see this house? (*pointing to the pavilion*) Ah, there, that path. I was running down there once, I remember... Yes, I remember. But, but… (*weeping*) I don't know any more than that. (*she collapses on the bench*)

(*Tom Brown and Toby return.*)

TOM BROWN (*seeing Kitty*): Ah! (*to Toby*) Keep a lookout.

TOBY: Right.

(*Toby walks away.*)

TOM BROWN (*going to Kitty*): Kitty?

KITTY (*rising and staying put*): Ah!

TOM BROWN: Don't you recognize me?

KITTY (*distracted*): Yes? (*then recoiling*) Yes!

TOM BROWN: What's wrong with you?

KITTY: Go away! Go away!

TOM BROWN: Go away from here? With you! Yes, let's leave.

KITTY (*recoiling*): Ah, don't come near me! Stay away!

TOM BROWN: Look, Kitty, you do recognize me, right? It's me, Tom Brown.

KITTY (*still distracted*): Tom Brown?

TOM BROWN: Yes!

KITTY (*repeating*): Tom Brown! (*after a pause*) Hold on! Listen to me.

TOM BROWN (*close to her*): What have you to tell me?

KITTY: You're going to know! You must know, right? Well, I fled the wretched hovel that was sheltering me. After two days of walking without knowing where I was going, sleeping in doorways, in parks, in thickets, I don't know how, but I got here. I was really hungry, and fell senseless before the gate where charitable people harbored me! All I had left was a penny. A single penny. I could have bread with that, right? But no, I used it to think of you, one more time. One last time. (*reaction by Tom Brown*) I didn't buy bread; instead, I bought this. (*she takes the newspaper and presents it to him*) Here, read that!

TOM BROWN: But…

KITTY: Read it, will you! Are you going to read it, since it speaks of you?

TOM BROWN: Kitty!

KITTY (*tossing away the newspaper*): You understand now, don't you? And you understand why I fled my hovel—Jack?

TOM BROWN (*recoiling*): Kitty!

KITTY (*striding toward him*): You're Jack the Ripper!

TOM BROWN: You know? Who told you?

KITTY: I saw you!

TOM BROWN: You! You saw me!

KITTY: Yes! Over your victim, striking her with your knife. I saw you do it, savage and hideous! I heard the monstrous words you uttered! I saw you, at last, fleeing, leaving the body of the wretched woman you had just slain.

TOM BROWN: Kitty, hear me!

KITTY: Ah! You have nothing more to say to me! I have nothing more to listen to!

TOM BROWN: All the same, you're going to listen to me! It's true! I struck her! But she was informing for Lestrade. And I took an oath, an oath I'll keep whatever happens, whatever it may cost me! An oath to strike down mercilessly all those who betray me!

KITTY: All?

TOM BROWN: All! That woman was spying on you too! Following you! Because of her, we were going to be arrested, separated forever! I didn't want that!

KITTY: And now?

TOM BROWN: And now? Now you're going to follow me.

KITTY (*resolutely*): Never!

TOM BROWN: Kitty!

KITTY (*moving away*): Never, I tell you! Get out of here! Get out of my sight!

TOM BROWN: You refuse to follow me?

KITTY: How can you ask that!

TOM BROWN: I could force you!

KITTY (*grabbing a knife from the table*): One more step and I'll kill myself right before your eyes.

TOM BROWN: Ah! (*terrified, recoiling*) No! A thousand times no!

KITTY (after a pause): Listen! There's still a way for us to remain together.

TOM BROWN: Speak! Tell me what must be done!

KITTY: You have on you the knife you used to commit your crimes? As for me, I've got this one here. Let's strike ourselves at the same time, as we look into each other's eyes, lips to lips. We'll be joined forever in eternity.

TOM BROWN: Die, at your age?

KITTY: It's not a question of me! I'm sacrificing my life to shield you from the punishment that awaits you—the scaffold that clamors for you. By dying with you, I am buying you a pardon. (*a pause*) Do you want it?

TOM BROWN: Kitty...

KITTY: Ah! He's afraid! He's afraid!

TOM BROWN: Well, yes, I'm afraid! The scaffold, you say? Right now, I'm able to protect myself from that! I love you! You belong to me! You're mine! I want you! But, I want you living.

(*Toby returns*.)

KITTY: You will only have me dead!

(*She raises the knife to kill herself. Toby rushes to her and snatches the knife away*.)

TOBY: Mustn't play with that, Miss, it's very sharp.

KITTY: Ah!

TOM BROWN (*rushing her*): Mine, Kitty! You are mine! Come!

(*He drags her away*.)

KITTY (*screaming*): Help! Help!

(*Sir William appears and rushes between her and Tom Brown*.)

SIR WILLIAM HUXELL: You are using violence with a woman? You are a coward, sir!

TOM BROWN (*roaring*): Ah! You! You'll pay for everything.

(*He grabs the knife from Toby's hand and attacks Sir William. Suddenly, Mr. Robinson enters from the left, revolver in hand, and leaps into the melee.*)

ROBINSON: One more step and you're dead!

KITTY: Goodbye, Tom Brown! I am going to wait for you.

(*She leaves, in tears.*)

ROBINSON (*to Tom Brown who had made a gesture of following her*): Don't budge. (*jestingly*) Milord, or should I say Tom Brown, I have the honor of informing you that I've caught you and I'm arresting you!

TOM BROWN (*taking a revolver from his pocket*): Get out of the way!

(*He fires at Robinson, who stumbles.*)

ROBINSON: Ah, the brigand!

(*He falls on the bench at the right.*)

SIR WILLIAM HUXELL: Wretch!

(*He starts to rush Tom Brown, who leaps over the gate, followed by Toby.*)

TOM BROWN (*to Robinson*): Not today! (*threatening Sir William with his revolver*) As for you, we'll meet again!

(*He vanishes with Toby.*)

SIR WILLIAM HUXELL (*returning to Robinson*): Are you wounded?

ROBINSON: In the shoulder. A scratch! It's really emotion!

(*Ellen returns, followed by her father.*)

ELLEN PLACK: Those shots! What's going on?

SIR WILLIAM HUXELL: That man, who introduced himself under the name of Lord Maxwell…

SIR JAMES PLACK: Yes?

SIR WILLIAM HUXELL: He's a bandit! He's…

ROBINSON (*rising*): He is—Jack the Ripper!

(*Nick Carter appears at the gate and rushes after Tom Brown and Toby.*)

C U R T A I N

## *SCENE V*

The courtyard of the Whitechapel police station. Another Sergeant and several women prostitutes.

SERGEANT (*calling the roll*): Elizabeth Jackson!

ELIZABETH JACKSON: Present.

SERGEANT: Jane Goodman!

JANE GOODMAN: Present!

SERGEANT: Anna Wilkins!

ANNA WILKINS: Present!

SERGEANT: Very good! I've got my count. You've been brought here to be questioned by the Inspector Lestrade himself.

ELIZABETH JACKSON: What's he want with us?

SERGEANT: Silence! You have no right to speak except when you are questioned.

(*Murmuring amongst the women. Constable Stone enters from the left.*)

STONE: The women are here?

SERGEANT: The fifth section, yes.

STONE: Fine! Inspector Lestrade has finished with the fourth section.

(*Lestrade enters from the right.*)

STONE: Here he is.

WOMEN (*curtsying to him*): Your Honor…

INSPECTOR LESTRADE: That's fine! That's fine! I have some good news for you all. Amongst others, a reward for those of you who give me the best information about a certain matter that you already know and have certainly discussed between you. (*approving murmurs*) Are you satisfied? (to Stone, giving him a list of names) Here, Mr. Stone, you will call the order beginning with the last comer.

STONE (*after taking the list*): Anna Wilkins.

(*Anna comes forward.*)

INSPECTOR LESTRADE: You are quite young. How old are you?

ANNA WILKINS: Eighteen

INSPECTOR LESTRADE: Your father?

ANNA WILKINS: Dead. Hanged at Newgate.

INSPECTOR LESTRADE: Your mother?

ANNA WILKINS: Dead, too. In hospital.

INSPECTOR LESTRADE: Of what illness?

ANNA WILKINS: She drank too much

INSPECTOR LESTRADE: Three women have just been murdered in three days in Whitechapel. Do you know about it?

ANNA WILKINS: How would I know about it?

INSPECTOR LESTRADE: True enough. You've been in here for a week. The first of these women was Mary Clarwick.

ANNA WILKINS: It's her lover—Tom Merwin—who must have done it; that man was jealous.

INSPECTOR LESTRADE: Tom Merwin was hanged ten days ago. He couldn't have murdered his mistress three nights ago. On the handle of the knife used to kill her was a crudely carved name—Jack the Ripper. Which of you has heard of that man? (*silence*) No one? (*to himself*) Just like the other sections. (*to Stone*) Continue.

STONE: Jane Goodman

(*Jane comes forward.*)

INSPECTOR LESTRADE: A month ago, you gave up your lover to me. He was part of the same gang as Merwin. He was hanged, just like his mate.

JANE GOODMAN: The poor man.

INSPECTOR LESTRADE: You were paid 20 pounds for that! It must have been almost a fortune for you. How does it happen that I find you here again?

JANE GOODMAN: Love!

INSPECTOR LESTRADE: You actually have a heart?

JANE GOODMAN: Ah, yes, To my misfortune. With my 20 pounds, I got myself loved by a gentleman of sorts. When I no longer had any money, he no longer loved me. I had to steal to eat. And they brought me here.

INSPECTOR LESTRADE: The second woman murdered by the man who styles himself Jack the Ripper was known as The Irish Girl.

JANE GOODMAN: Colleen! (*horrified*) She was my best friend! And she's dead, too?

INSPECTOR LESTRADE: Yes. Brutally murdered. She never spoke to you of Jack?

JANE GOODMAN: No! Her lover was named Cross. He was hanged a while back.

INSPECTOR LESTRADE: This Cross, wasn't he friends with Tom Merwin?

JANE GOODMAN: They never left each other.

INSPECTOR LESTRADE (*aside*): So that's really it. This string of crimes against the women who've given up their lovers is simply the result of an act of vengeance. They denounced their lovers. They will die. (*to Jane*) You may go. (*to Stone*) Continue.

STONE: Elizabeth Jackson.

(*Elizabeth steps forward.*)

INSPECTOR LESTRADE: The name of the last victim is Lucy Brown. Did you know her ?

ELIZABETH JACKSON: Sure. She, too, had denounced her lover, who was hanged like the others.

INSPECTOR LESTRADE: He was hanged six days ago. You've been in here for two weeks. How do you know he was hanged?

ELIZABETH JACKSON (*embarrassed*): Hell !

INSPECTOR LESTRADE: Answer, or you'll spend two weeks here—in solitary.

ELIZABETH JACKSON: I read it in the newspapers.

INSPECTOR LESTRADE: You get newspapers in here?

ELIZABETH JACKSON: There was some paper lying around. I picked it up.

INSPECTOR LESTRADE (*to the Sergeant*): Come here, you. Why didn't you see this scrap of paper on the ground?

SERGEANT: I dunno.

INSPECTOR LESTRADE: Why didn't you see this woman pick it up?

SERGEANT: I dunno.

INSPECTOR LESTRADE: You'll be do ten days in Southwick prison.

SERGEANT: But…

INSPECTOR LESTRADE: Enough! That's too much! They're in jail and they read newspapers! What kind of station is this?

(*Constable Trent enters from the back.*)

TRENT: Sir, you told me to bring you all the telegrams and important letters that arrived in your absence. Here they are.

INSPECTOR LESTRADE: Fine. (*to the Sergeant*) Take these women back to their cells.

SERGEANT (*to women*): Come along, the lot of you

(*All the women curtsy to Inspector Lestrade.*)

INSPECTOR LESTRADE: Good day!

(*The Sergeant makes the women leave and shuts the gate behind him.*)

INSPECTOR LESTRADE: Let's see these letters… (*opening one and perusing it*) From Lord Melbourne who offers to put his two mastiffs at my disposal to patrol Whitechapel with detectives. (*gives the letter back to Trent*) We'll see. (*opening second letter*) A note from Sherlock Holmes who informs me he's beginning his investigation into the Whitechapel murders as of this evening. (*taking the third letter*) A gentleman who asks my permission to dress as a woman and walk at night in Whitechapel as a decoy… Is that all?

TRENT: That's all.

INSPECTOR LESTRADE: What about Betty Blackthorn?

TRENT: She's locked up here. (*pointing to the right*)

INSPECTOR LESTRADE: Has she talked yet?

TRENT: No, sir.

INSPECTOR LESTRADE: She will talk! She must!

(*Mr. Robinson, dressed as a policeman, looking very wet, tries to enter but is stopped by the Sergeant.*)

ROBINSON: Will you let me in! I am a detective! Do you understand? An amateur—but a detective nevertheless! (*seeing Lestrade, he manages to push the Sergeant aside and enters.*)

ROBINSON: Inspector Lestrade!

INSPECTOR LESTRADE (*aside*): This imbecile again!

ROBINSON (*drying his face*): God, how hot I feel! It must be a reaction to all the emotions. (*to Lestrade*) How am I doing? Very well, thank you!.

INSPECTOR LESTRADE (*frowning*): What?

ROBINSON: When I say "very well," perhaps I'm exaggerating. But my wound has healed quite a bit.

INSPECTOR LESTRADE: What wound?

ROBINSON: Didn't you know? Jack the Ripper shot me.

INSPECTOR LESTRADE: You saw him?

ROBINSON: As I am looking at you. A handsome man! A swine, certainly—but a handsome man.

INSPECTOR LESTRADE: Look here! You must be mad…

ROBINSON: No. I am lucid. Being wet makes me extra-lucid. And I am here with the Little Virgin.

INSPECTOR LESTRADE: The Little Virgin? Kitty?

ROBINSON: Yes. She was recognized on the docks. He called her by that name, so I suppose that it is hers. I've brought her to you.

INSPECTOR LESTRADE: Why?

ROBINSON (*drying his face again*): I'm too out of breath to tell you… She's at the station, changing clothes. Damn, a dip in the Thames can really soak you!

INSPECTOR LESTRADE: I don't understand! Explain yourself more clearly.

ROBINSON: I wasn't clear? Well, here I go again. I was stretched out in Sir James' garden, in broad daylight, when an uproar of voices struck my ear. I listened and I heard a conversation. The kind of conversation that makes your hair stand on end--if one has any, because if one doesn't…

INSPECTOR LESTRADE: Come to the point, will you! Who was talking?

ROBINSON: Who? But the very gentleman who had a bit of fight with you earlier and had criticized your police work!

INSPECTOR LESTRADE: So he came back?

ROBINSON: Yes, with his lad. Oh, that lad—I recognized him. He was my magnetizer! Anyway, the gentleman was talking with a young girl…

INSPECTOR LESTRADE: Ah!

ROBINSON: She told him she was leaving him because she'd seen him murder a woman! She showed him a newspaper and she said: "Read this, Jack the Ripper!"

INSPECTOR LESTRADE: Are you certain?

ROBINSON: As certain as I was asleep.

INSPECTOR LESTRADE: But this young girl who was talking with that man…

ROBINSON: As I told you: it was the Little Virgin. Then, she fled. The man tried to follow her and he shot at me! Bang! He missed—or almost. I fired back. I missed, too. Two shots were exchanged without results, or almost without results. He ran away! I rushed in pursuit, but, Hell, he had a leg up on me, the cur! I ran towards the Thames. I reached the banks just when the Little Virgin, whom I recognized from a distance, threw herself into the river. If my legs are not good perpendicularly, it's quite another matter horizontally. I swim like a fish—all fat men swim well. Plop! I took a header! I reached the young girl. I grabbed her. I pulled her to the river bank, and the nearest place to get help was the Whitechapel Police Station, so I brought her here. They told me I would find you in the courtyard. I came here, and that's the whole story! You don't have any brandy by any chance? No? Then I might die…

INSPECTOR LESTRADE: You did all this?

ROBINSON: My God, yes, I did all this! I'd give up my 20,000 pounds for some brandy right now! As I was drenched, a brave policeman offered me his uniform to dry off. I gratefully accepted his offer! He's in his underwear at the station. I'm going to send it back to him as soon as I go and change.

INSPECTOR LESTRADE: Mr. Robinson, you are a brave man!

ROBINSON: I know that well enough. But just tell me I'm in it.

INSPECTOR LESTRADE: In what?

ROBINSON: In the police!

INSPECTOR LESTRADE: With pleasure! With enthusiasm you're in it!

ROBINSON: With enthusiasm? I've stirred enthusiasm in you! Long live Inspector Lestrade!

INSPECTOR LESTRADE (*to Trent*): Have the young girl that Master Robinson just came with brought here.

(*Trent leaves*.)

INSPECTOR LESTRADE: You were telling me that this young girl…

ROBINSON: …Is as pure as spring water.

INSPECTOR LESTRADE: All the same, she's the mistress of this murderer!

ROBINSON: She disowned him, Inspector! She disowned him, knife in hand! Still, I might be mistaken in saying she's as pure as spring water. Let's say, pure as Thames water.

(*Trent and two policemen help Kitty in.*)

INSPECTOR LESTRADE (*to Kitty*): Come in, come in, child!

(*The two policemen leave.*)

KITTY: Why did they save me? Why didn't they let me die?

INSPECTOR LESTRADE: Because you must live, Kitty! Live for those who love you!

KITTY: No one loves me! And why would anyone love me?

INSPECTOR LESTRADE (*to Trent*): Mr. Trent, please telephone Sir James Plack and ask him to come and see me at the Whitechapel police station.

TRENT: Right, sir.

(*He leaves by the back.*)

INSPECTOR LESTRADE (*to Kitty*): No one loves you, you say. Not even—*him*?

KITTY: *Him*? Who's that? Who are you talking about?

INSPECTOR LESTRADE: I'm talking about Jack.

KITTY: Jack?

INSPECTOR LESTRADE: Jack the Ripper. The Whitechapel murderer.

KITTY: Why talk to me about that man? I don't know him.

INSPECTOR LESTRADE: You do know him; he's your lover.

KITTY: Who says that?

INSPECTOR LESTRADE (*pointing to Robinson*): This gentleman.

ROBINSON: Ah, pardon me!

INSPECTOR LESTRADE: You just told me, yes or no?

ROBINSON: Well, I told you, but I didn't mean to.

INSPECTOR LESTRADE (*severely*): Mr. Robinson!

ROBINSON: Ah, but when I told you, I didn't know that it might hurt this little darling. If it does, I withdraw what I said. (*going to Kitty and placing his arm around her*)

KITTY: Thank you, sir! Oh, you are good! But why did you snatch me from death? (*she weeps*)

ROBINSON (*moved*): I… I don't know. It was a long time since I'd taken a bath… (*he dries his eyes*)

INSPECTOR LESTRADE: Kitty, come closer. (*she does*) You have a family…

KITTY: A family? Me?

INSPECTOR LESTRADE: Yes. A father and a sister who are trying to find you. They want you!

KITTY: My God!

INSPECTOR LESTRADE: I can release you into their hands, but only if you tell me who is the man known by the name of Jack the Ripper.

KITTY: Ah! What are you asking of me!

INSPECTOR LESTRADE: I'm asking you to give up your lover! A wretched murderer! In exchange, I'll give you a fortune, a name, and relatives who will cherish you.

KITTY: I've never known my father. If he were to meet me, he'd probably blush in embarrassment. I don't want to see him. I won't talk.

INSPECTOR LESTRADE: Take care!...

ROBINSON: Ah! You're not going to threaten her?

INSPECTOR LESTRADE: My friend, I advise you not to meddle in things that don't concern you.

ROBINSON: But, sir, this does concern me. I saved this young girl's life!

INSPECTOR LESTRADE: Let's try this… (*to Kitty*) Kitty, get back inside. (*pointing to the right*) I will give you a quarter of an hour to think about my offer. (*to Robinson*) Mr. Robinson, talk to her and try to convince her. It's a question of apprehending a monster, not of the happiness of this poor child.

ROBINSON: Of her happiness! That decides me! (*to Kitty*) Come, Miss Kitty!

KITTY (*to herself*): Give him up? Never!

ROBINSON: So long as I don't doze off, catechizing her.

(*They leave.*)

STONE: She won't talk.

INSPECTOR LESTRADE: Betty will talk for her. Bring her here.

(*Stone nods and leaves.*)

INSPECTOR LESTRADE (*alone*): She's Sir James' daughter! That scar on her face, her story, everything confirms it. Betty will remove any last doubts.

(*Stone returns, pushing Betty Blackthorn before him.*)

STONE: Come in, get in here!

BETTY BLACKTHORN (*yawning*): Ah, at last! I can see you! I've got 'em, I've know everything!

INSPECTOR LESTRADE: Then, talk!

BETTY BLACKTHORN: Having returned to Whitechapel by your order, I found myself facing a man I've sworn to avenge myself on. He threw me in the bottom of a cellar. I expected to die! He promised me that! Two of his men were guarding me, talking to themselves. It's through these men that I learned the name of their leader: Tom Brown! It's through them that I learned the place where they meet every night: under the Southwick bridge. I'll take you there, tonight, at 3 o'clock! The men got tired of waiting, and left me there. Alone in that cellar. God, I'm thirsty.

INSPECTOR LESTRADE: Do you want some gin?

BETTY BLACKTHORN: No! I won't remember, and I want to remember! Where was I? Ah, yes! Little by little, my eyes got used to the darkness, and I discovered a trapdoor. It was my salvation!. But how to get it open? I tried breaking it open, but I wasn't strong enough. I tried to pull out the nails, the iron work, but my nails broke. I was going to give up, when suddenly, my feet bumped into something. It was like an iron bar. I bent over and picked it up. It was a pair of tongs. I grasped it and attacked the door with the rage of despair. I eventually got the bolt loose. I was saved! At least, I thought so. But there were many more dangers in store yet. This trapdoor gave onto a tunnel. There, there was only darkness, and, in the distance, from time to time, the terrifying sound of trains. I could have been run over a hundred times! At last, I got out of that hell alive! I saw daylight and I ran here to say to you: Inspector Lestrade, this very night, thanks to me, you will capture the whole gang of malefactors who are infesting London.

INSPECTOR LESTRADE: Fine! Excellent! Betty, tell me, this man, this Tom Brown, didn't he mention his mistress to you?

BETTY BLACKTHORN: Kitty, you mean? Yes, he questioned me about her past.

INSPECTOR LESTRADE: Ah-ah!

BETTY BLACKTHORN: But I didn't tell him a thing. It's because he understood that my answers were lies that he wanted to kill me.

INSPECTOR LESTRADE: And what about me? Are you going to lie to me too?

BETTY BLACKTHORN: Perish the thought!

(*Trent returns accompanied by Sir James Plack, his daughter and Sir William Huxell.*)

TRENT: Sir, here's Sir James.

SIR JAMES PLACK: You've asked for me, Inspector Lestrade, and I came running.

INSPECTOR LESTRADE: Yes! I've got some good news! Listen to what this woman is going to say. (To Berry) Come on, Betty, speak!

BETTY BLACKTHORN: First of all, my name isn't Betty Blackthorn.

INSPECTOR LESTRADE: Ah?

BETTY BLACKTHORN: yes. My real name is Victoria Trevor.

SIR JAMES PLACK (*uttering a cry*): Oh! You're the one who stole my Clary!

BETTY BLACKTHORN: Ah?

SIR JAMES PLACK (*grabbing Betty's collar and shaking her*): Confess! Confess, will you!

SIR WILLIAM HUXELL: Sir James, please, I entreat you…

INSPECTOR LESTRADE: Let him alone, let him speak.

SIR JAMES PLACK: Answer! Were you her nurse?

BETTY BLACKTHORN: Yes.

SIR JAMES PLACK: What did you do with her? Tell me what became of her? Tell me, or else…

BETTY BLACKTHORN (*not easily intimidated*): Ah, I don't owe you any account!

SIR JAMES PLACK: What? You don't owe me an account? (*ready to strangle her*)

BETTY BLACKTHORN: No, I don't! Who are you to talk to me like this?

SIR JAMES PLACK: Who am I?

BETTY BLACKTHORN: Yes!

SIR JAMES PLACK: I'm her father!

BETTY BLACKTHORN: Ah!

SIR JAMES PLACK: You understand now why I'm questioning you, right? You understand now why I'm in haste to know the truth?

BETTY BLACKTHORN (*lowering her head*): Yes.

SIR JAMES PLACK: Why did you steal my child from me? Speak? Why? Why?

BETTY BLACKTHORN (*somberly*): Because I was a mother, too, and they stole my son from me. Because I wanted to get back at the world and make another woman suffer the tortures that I had endured.

SIR JAMES PLACK: But my daughter… What did you do with her?

BETTY BLACKTHORN: I sent her to beg. A long time later!

SIR JAMES PLACK (*savagely*): You wretch!

BETTY BLACKTHORN (*bowing her head*): Ah, it was an evil thing to do... Now, I repent.

SIR JAMES PLACK: She repents! And that's all she is able to say! She repents! I'm suffering the tortures of Hell and she repents! To appease my soul, I must know everything. I order you to talk! What's become of my daughter?

BETTY BLACKTHORN: I don't know. She left me.

SIR JAMES PLACK: But you've seen her? You know where she is?

INSPECTOR LESTRADE: No need to question her further, Sir James, I will tell you the rest.

SIR JAMES PLACK: You?

INSPECTOR LESTRADE: Yes. (*to Trent and Stone, pointing at Betty*) Take her away.

SIR JAMES PLACK: Take her away? No! You can't! I forbid it!

INSPECTOR LESTRADE: Please, sir!

ELLEN PLACK: Father!

SIR WILLIAM HUXELL: Sir James.

INSPECTOR LESTRADE (*to Trent and Stone*): Go!

BETTY BLACKTHORN: But will I be set free this evening?

INSPECTOR LESTRADE: Why should you?

BETTY BLACKTHORN (*savagely*): To see him again! To have my revenge on Tom Brown!

INSPECTOR LESTRADE: That's fine. Yes, you will be set free for that. I promise you.

BETTY BLACKTHORN: Ah, I'll be even with him! (*to Trent and Stone*) I can't wait! Come on, move!

(*They leave*.)

SIR JAMES PLACK: Did I hear you right, Inspector Lestrade? You can return my daughter to me? You know where she is?

INSPECTOR LESTRADE: Yes.

ELLEN PLACK: Ah, father! You see plainly you were wrong to doubt God!

INSPECTOR LESTRADE (*at the door to the right*): Come in, Miss!

(*Kitty enters excitedly, followed by Mr. Robinson*.)

KITTY: I heard everything! (*very moved, looking at Ellen*) So! This beautiful young lady, so noble, so generous, is sister to poor Kitty?

ELLEN PLACK: Why, it's the young girl we helped! Do you recognize her, William?

SIR WILLIAM HUXLEY: Certainly!

SIR JAMES PLACK (*to Lestrade*): This child… It is she, right? She's my daughter?

KITTY (*excitedly*): No, sir! No! I don't have that happiness!

INSPECTOR LESTRADE: But…

KITTY (*cutting him off*): Ah, Inspector Lestrade knows quite well I am not Kitty! But he must have told you that I knew her. That's the truth.

SIR JAMES PLACK: That you knew her?

INSPECTOR LESTRADE (*impatiently*): Come on, child…

KITTY (*rushing to Lestrade and pulling him aside*): For pity's sake, sir, shut up. You know quite well what I am: a girl of the streets. To unmask me to them is to dishonor their house. This young man will flee his fiancée. This pure young girl will die of despair. My father will be crushed by shame! Have pity on them! Don't strike them down! I beg you!

INSPECTOR LESTRADE (*preventing her from kneeling, after a pause*): Okay. I'll keep my mouth shut.

KITTY (*low*): Thank you, thank you! (*returning to Sir James*) Inspector Lestrade was about to tell you that I knew her, your child. Alas, she was very unhappy.

SIR JAMES PLACK: Where is she? What happened to her?

KITTY (*very simply*): Heavens! She is dead!

ALL: Dead!

KITTY: Yes, quite dead!

SIR JAMES PLACK: My daughter is dead? Oh, no, no! That's not possible! God would not have given her back to me and taken her away at the same time!

KITTY: I saw her die with my own eyes.

SIR JAMES PLACK: Ah, Lord! Lord! You are without pity! (*he collapses into a chair*)

KITTY: I held her head, here, in my arms and she grasped my hand, feeling death approach. Suddenly, she said to me, as if by chance: "Should you ever meet those who gave me life, tell them that I really would have loved them with all my heart." She gave me a last kiss and her soul flew to be with God's angels. That kiss I received from her, would you allow me to pass it on to you, sir?

SIR JAMES PLACK (*bawling*): Yes, yes!

KITTY (*running to him*): These are the lips that touched her face! It's her kiss I am giving you. (*she kisses him*)

ELLEN PLACK (*going to her*): Miss, let me touch your hand, the hand that held hers. I love you as I would have loved her.

KITTY: She would have pressed you to her heart! (*she kisses her passionately, then pulls away*) Ah, no, no! This is too much. Goodbye! Goodbye!

(*She flees to the back.*)

INSPECTOR LESTRADE: Follow her, Mr. Robinson.

ROBINSON: I won't lose sight of her! Ah, what a brave girl!

CURTAIN

## *ACT IV*

### *SCENE VI*

The Southwick Bridge seen obliquely from left to far back right. To the left, there is the mouth of a sewer, blocked by an iron grill. To the side, there is a stone stairway leading from the bridge to the shore. It can also be entered from the right. We see a perspective of London in the rear. It is night. From time to time, moonlight illuminates the scene.

AT RISE, a boat is seen with two men in it, approaching from the left, and landing against the pylon of the bridge at the right. Two men disembark and step forward with the utmost precaution. Suddenly, they find themselves lit by a ray of moonlight. Only then we recognize Sir William Huxell and Mr. Robinson, still wearing his police uniform.

ROBINSON: We're in plenty of light.

(*They abruptly hurry into the darkness at the right.*)

SIR WILLIAM HUXLEY: Are you sure that this is the right place? Under the Southwick bridge?

ROBINSON: Where the gang is going to meet? Of course! That's what Betty Blackthorn herself told Inspector Lestrade.

SIR WILLIAM HUXLEY: But Inspector Lestrade isn't here?

ROBINSON: We're ahead of him by two hours at least. Perhaps, we were wrong. We would have done better to come in force. But you were in such a hurry…

SIR WILLIAM HUXLEY: The violent emotion Sir James experienced was such that he became suddenly ill when he got home. What do Jack the Ripper and his gang mean to me? Nothing! What concerns me is that young girl! It's she that I am in haste to see again.

ROBINSON: Do you think that…?

SIR WILLIAM HUXLEY: I think that I can still restore a young girl to her father, and that it's through Kitty that I will succeed in accomplishing that miracle. You went in pursuit of her. What happened?

ROBINSON: I was tired already. She's got quite a leg, that girl! I dozed off by Cleopatra's needle. A charitable soul seeing a policeman dozing led me back to Scotland Yard, where you were still with Inspector Lestrade. You told me that it was absolutely necessary to find Kitty, so we've come here.

SIR WILLIAM HUXLEY: But what if she doesn't come?

ROBINSON: It's only one o'clock. She will come, don't doubt that. Have confidence in my flair!

SIR WILLIAM HUXLEY (*cocking an ear*): Hark!

ROBINSON: I heard a noise too! Brr! Now I regret we came!

SIR WILLIAM HUXLEY (*pulling him to the side*): Come here and let's observe!

ROBINSON: OK!

(*They withdraw into the shadows*.)

(*Having crossed the bridge, Toby comes down the stone stairway, looking in every direction*.)

TOBY (*to himself*): Nobody? I seem to be first. None of the others are here yet. Let's wait.

(*Moon light*.)

ROBINSON (*head appearing*): Why, unless I'm mistaken, it's my magnetizer.

TOBY (*to himself*): Ah, we got away handily from Sir James Plack's place! I really thought we were going to be nabbed!

ROBINSON (*aside*): My, my! (*to Sir William*) Should we begin with him?

SIR WILLIAM HUXLEY: No. Wait.

TOBY (*to himself*): Still, it was worth the risk. We had time to examine the place and, tonight, that young Miss Ellen will be carried away like a feather.

SIR WILLIAM HUXLEY (*stunned*): What do I hear?

TOBY: That's not nasty work. Kidnappings are more my style.

ROBINSON (*low to Sir William*): Watch and don't try to stop me. I have a score to settle with that little rascal.

SIR WILLIAM HUXLEY: But…

ROBINSON: Don't be afraid. I'm quite strong. This won't take long.

(*Sir William's head disappears.*)

TOBY (*takes a pipe from his pocket and lit it*): There's one fellow that I'd like to see again—that fat fool, Robinson. Ah, if I run across him again…

ROBINSON (*who's approached him quietly, tapping him on the shoulder*): Yoo-hoo! Here I am! Good evening, my dear friend!

TOBY (*takings a step back and putting himself on the defensive*): You!

ROBINSON (*pretending to shoot magnetic fluid at him*): Don't move! You're in my power now!

TOBY: Really, fat man? You'll see who is in whose power!

ROBINSON (*shooting fluid at him again*): I told you not to move. You are nervous. I am calm. Since mind has more influence on the human body than nerves, I easily dominate you.

TOBY: Huh? What are you talking about? (*assuming a boxing stance*) See these fists?

ROBINSON: Ah! You want to box? At that game, my little friend, you'll be sorry.

(*After two or three passes, Toby is hit hard. Robinson grabs him by the collar.*)

ROBINSON: I told you not to move, didn't I?

TOBY: Help! Help!

ROBINSON: Don't shout! Don't try to struggle, or I'll fall on you and crush you.

TOBY (*trembling*): But what is it that you want?

ROBINSON: You'll find out soon enough. (*calling*) Sir William!

SIR WILLIAM HUXLEY (*appearing*): I'm here!

ROBINSON: Help me gag this young rascal.

TOBY (*struggling*): No! No!

ROBINSON: I've got him!

TOBY (*choking*): Ah!

(*Sir William pulls a kerchief from his pocket and ties it around Toby's mouth.*)

ROBINSON: Now, tie him up

(*Sir William ties Toby with a rope that Robinson wore around his belly.*)

ROBINSON: Ah, don't struggle, my lad!

TOBY (*in a strangled voice*): help!

SIR WILLIAM HUXLEY: It's done!

ROBINSON: Fine! Ah, see how sweet he is now! You'd swear he was a York ham. Now, we're going to place him in that boat…

SIR WILLIAM HUXLEY: But I want to stay here.

ROBINSON: Don't worry. We'll be right back. I'll carry him. (*carrying Toby*) Go first and light the way, please. (*to Toby*) Well, my young swain, how about this for revenge? You see what happens! Let's be on our way.

(*The two men step into the boat, Robinson still carrying Toby, then vanish into the night. At this moment, a squad of militia cross the bridge from the left.*

(*After the soldiers have disappeared, the grill at the sewer's entrance opens and Tom Brown emerges. He then shuts the grill and places the key on a rock. He looks attentively at the soldiers who disappear on the right.*)

TOM BROWN: A round of militia the night of our party… But they're going. Nothing to worry about…

(*Two o'clock strikes.*)

TOM BROWN: Two o'clock. My companions should be here soon. Why isn't Toby already here? He must be drinking at the tavern. (*after a pause*) This is singular. Never have I experienced what I am experiencing today. This solitude almost frightens me! It seems to me that I'm all alone on this Earth. What's the matter with me? (*another pause*) What's wrong with me? Ah, I know! (*sitting on a large stone, with a dull cry of rage*) Ah! (*head in his hands*) She pushed me away! She hates me! And I love her more than ever! She fled. What's become of her? Kitty! Kitty! (*raising his head*) Why can't I drive this stupid passion out of my heart? It twines about me! It burns me. It suffocates me. (*another pause*) Kitty knows now who I am. After I took so much care to hide it from her! I understand that she hates me.

(*A chuckling sound can be heard; it's a signal.*)

TOM BROWN: My associates! How welcome they are! With them, perhaps I'll forget. To forget... Anything for that.

(*Bartlett and a dozen of the gang, including women. appear.*)

BARTLETT: Can we come in?

TOM BROWN: There's nothing to fear.

(*Some enter from different directions.*)

RICKFORD (*coming down the stairway from the bridge*): Hey, fellas! Have a whiff of this! (*pointing to a big York ham*)

ALL: A ham!

BARTLETT (*taking it and examining it*): And real York pork! I know about such things.

(*Other men and women enter from all sides.*)

TOM BROWN: Where did you scout that out?

RICKFORD: At the door of a grocer.

TOPPS (*coming in*): What about this here bird ?

ALL: A roast chicken!

MERSON: And six pounds of roast beef that I pilfered at the home of one of our most excellent cook shops!

ALL: Hurrah!

DRUNKEN WOMAN: As for me, I cannot eat unless I've got something to drink.

ALL: Yes, yes, she's right! Something to drink!

BARTLETT: Keep it down, will you!

TOM BROWN: Bah! The last patrol has already passed.

BARTLETT: Oh, in that case, we're fine!

TOM BROWN: Merson, go to the store room, raise the slab and bring a dozen bottles of port and gin.

MERSON: Come help me, Mr. Topps.

TOPPS: With pleasure, Mr. Merson!

(*Merson and Topps exit under the pylon of the bridge.*)

TOM BROWN: Let's drink! Let's get drunk! (*to himself*) Perhaps that way, I'll manage to forget her!

(*All sit down . Rickford, in the midst of a group, slices up his ham and distributes shares. Bartlett does the same with his chicken and roast beef.*)

BARTLETT: And you, Tom Brown, you brought nothing along?

TOM BROWN: No.

RICKFORD: Today's Sunday and Tom Brown never works on Sunday.

TOM BROWN (to himself): How I suffer! What if Kitty left me for someone else? Yes! She must have! Someone else will replace her. But no—I love her. I'll tell her…

(*Topps returns with Merson, carrying bottles.*)

TOPPS: Here's the gin!

ALL: Hurrah!

BARTLETT: Uncork this for me, my lad.

TOPPS: I didn't wait for you to ask, Mr. Bartlett. It's done already!

MERSON: Pass your crystal, everyone!

(*All take from their pockets a bowl, a broken cup, a goblet, and hold them to Merson and Topps who pour out the drinks.*)

BARTLETT (*presenting a cup to Tom Brown*): For you, Mr. Tom Brown.

TOM BROWN: For me? To drink? Yes. (*he empties the cup, laughing nervously*) Ah, ah! Give me another. (*they refill his glass; he drinks*)

TOPPS: What a swig!

MERSON: Now there's something to see!

TOM BROWN: Gang, I'm announcing to you that I'm now a widower.

ALL: Ah, bah!

TOM BROWN: Yes. Kitty's left me. Henceforth she's dead to me! I no longer want anyone to mention her name to me, you hear? I don't want any more of her! She's an ingrate! I helped her, cared for her, saved her, and yet I no longer count for her. Ah, women are cowards! Gimme something to drink! Some gin! It's necessary to forget her. Quite necessary. Ah, Kitty! I hate you, I hate you! Pour more gin, will you! You can see plainly that I'm still thinking about her! (*they pour him more gin and he empties the glass with a gulp*)

BARTLETT: Bah! You're not the type of man to take a vow of celibacy.

TOM BROWN: No, by Jove! And I will soon prove it to you. (*after a pause, changing tone*) Ah, actually, there are too many of us here. I've got a job to put together for tonight. I want to be alone with my trusted assistants. (*murmurs*) Ah, there's also been too much murmuring lately. If that continues, I can work alone.

ALL: No, no!

TOM BROWN: Then shut up and go! Wait for us nearby. We have something to do tonight.

ALL: Goodbye, Tom Brown!

(*They exit by different sides.*)

TOM BROWN: Any bad news I should know?

BARTLETT: No! London is in revolt. Jack the Ripper terrifies the town.

TOM BROWN: That will give those disposed to denounce us something to think about.

RICKFORD: Who will be the next one to perish?

TOM BROWN: Betty Cross.

MERSON: When will that be?

TOM BROWN: Tomorrow night. But let's get back to tonight's business. I'll get into the place. I'll carry off the girl and I'll take her…

TOPPS: Where?

TOM BROWN: To the house in Euston Square.

BARTLETT: And then?

TOM BROWN: And then—her father's millions will ransom his daughter!

MERSON: How will you proceed?

TOM BROWN: I've explored the neighborhood. A surrounding wall protects the garden. It can easily be scaled. Once in the garden, it's no more than child's play. The grill will be opened. I'll answer for the young girl who will probably be nice enough to faint, and will be only easier to carry off. (*To Bartlett*) You will wait for me with a carriage nearby.

BARTLETT: Fine.

TOM BROWN: You know the address?

BARTLETT: By Jove, the home of Sir James Plack.

TOM BROWN: But why is it that Toby isn't here?

(*Kitty enters, going onto the bridge. She walks slowly, leaning over the parapet from time to time to look at the shore. Suddenly, she notices the group in the shadows.*)

BARTLETT (*replying to Tom Brown*): Hopefully, he wasn't nabbed.

KITTY (*from the middle of the bridge, calling in a low tone*): Tom Brown!

TOM BROWN (*starting*): Ah!

(*The men are terrified and flatten on the ground.*)

KITTY: Tom Brown!

TOM BROWN: Why, it's her voice! Kitty! Kitty!

KITTY: Yes, it's me! Wait for me!

(*She hurries across the bridge.*)

TOM BROWN: It's she! Here! She's coming!

BARTLETT (*rising*): I thought you no longer loved her?

MERSON (*getting up*): That you hated her?

TOM BROWN: Idiots! I adore her!

BARTLETT: Watch out, Tom Brown!

TOM BROWN: For what?

BARTLETT: I am wary of her! I really am!

TOM BROWN: You're mad!

BARTLETT: Who knows?

(*Kitty has come down the stairs from the bridge*.)

KITTY: Tom Brown!

TOM BROWN (*going to her*): You! You, at last!

KITTY (*stopping him with a gesture*): Wait! (*pointing to the bandits*) Who are these men?

TOM BROWN: They're my friends.

KITTY: Your friends. That means your gang, right?

TOM BROWN: Kitty!

KITTY: Yes! Bandits like you! That's what I wanted. Listen! Here's what I'm coming to do here...

TOM BROWN (*aside, uneasily*): What's wrong with her?

KITTY: Listen to me, Tom Brown! I'm weary of life. I no longer want to live. Life is a burden to me. And I'm too much a coward to kill myself…

TOM BROWN: Those ideas of suicide are haunting you again, Kitty! I beg you not to talk that way anymore!

KITTY: This morning, I tried to kill myself. (*horrified reaction by Tom Brown*) Ah! You didn't know? I'm going to tell you! I threw myself into the Thames. Ah, I had courage this morning, I was brave. I no longer am tonight.

TOM BROWN: You wanted to drown?

KITTY: Yes. But they saved me. I wanted to start again just now. Well, this time, courage failed me. This large dark stream of water frightened me. (*shivering*) No, no! I couldn't!

TOM BROWN: Kitty, please…

KITTY: And still, I must die!

TOM BROWN: Why?

KITTY: Because I don't want to be a murderer's lover!

TOM BROWN: Wretch!

KITTY: Yes! I saw you! You know it very well! I've got to die because you've ruined me! Because I love you despite everything! Because you'll drag me lower still. And I don't want to plunge any deeper in the muck.

TOM BROWN: Kitty…

KITTY: You wanted me to speak. I've spoken.

TOM BROWN: You are without pity.

KITTY (*aside*): Pity! He dares to speak to me of pity! Him! The murderer!

(*Murmurs from the men.*)

TOM BROWN: Ah, shut up, the rest of you!

KITTY: Not having the courage to kill myself, I came here to get myself killed by you.

TOM BROWN: By me?

KITTY: Or by your men. It doesn't make any difference to me.

TOM BROWN: You know that everyone here respects you, and…

KITTY: We'll see about that! Didn't you all take an oath?

TOM BROWN: An oath?

KITTY The one about mercilessly killing women who betrayed you?

TOM BROWN: How do you know?

KITTY: You told me! And then, two nights ago, didn't I see you crouching over the body of the Irish Girl, ripping her with your knife, saying, "This is how Jack the Ripper takes vengeance!" Well, kill me then—because I denounced you!

TOM BROWN: What?

KITTY: I denounced all of you.

ALL (*rushing at her*): Let's kill her!

TOM BROWN (*placing himself in front of her*): Stop! She's lying! She's saying that because she wants us to kill her. She's lying. I swear to you, she's lying!

KITTY: No! I'm not lying! Inspector Lestrade and his men will be here any moment.

ALL: Let's kill her!

TOM BROWN: I tell you, I don't want this!

BARTLETT: You haven't the right to oppose it.

ALL: Yes, yes! Death to her!

TOM BROWN (*pulling out a gun*): The first one to step forward dies!

(*They recoil.*)

KITTY: Ah! Cowards! You're afraid. Strike me, will you! Kill me! Haven't you understood yet? I've betrayed you, I've denounced you! They're coming and they're going to arrest you! They're going to hang you! Avenge yourselves, you cowards! Cowards, cowards, cowards!

TOM BROWN: Leave me alone with her. I tell you that she's crazy, she's lying! She loves me. You heard her tell me so! Do you send to death the one you love? Did I just kill her? I tell you—no, I order you to leave me alone with her.

BARTLETT: We're here, ready to leave, but not before striking her down if it turns out she's been telling the truth.

(*The gang disappears.*)

TOM BROWN: Kitty, admit that you lied.

KITTY: I told the truth.

TOM BROWN: You've denounced us?

KITTY: Yes.

TOM BROWN: Swear to me!

KITTY: I swear to you. Now, kill me and run away. They're coming at three o'clock. You've got plenty of time.

TOM BROWN: I've been denounced by you? Swear that as well!

KITTY: By me—or by someone else! What does it matter! They're going to come and arrest you. It's death for you if you stay here. Now kill me before they get here, and then get away fast. It's your only chance.

TOM BROWN: You see quite well that you're lying. Give me up to the cops, you? If I had betrayed you, you wouldn't have done it. You love me as I love you! I feel it through what I experience myself. If I saw you in the arms of another man, I'd kill you, but I wouldn't give you up to the police.

KITTY: Tom Brown, I beg you to do it. Take pity on me. Free me from life! And as your dagger enters my heart, my lips will give you one last kiss.

TOM BROWN: Kitty, we can still live happily together.

KITTY: Happily! You dare to think it!

TOM BROWN: I am going to be rich, very rich.

KITTY: Through a new crime, right?

TOM BROWN: No! There's been enough blood shed. No more killing! With this fortune that I will soon control, we can leave England, hide in some corner of the world where we will live only for each other, unknown to all.

KITTY: Unknown to all? Except to ourselves. That's too much!

TOM BROWN: Kitty, I beseech you. On my knees! See! I am dragging myself to your feet. Come! We'll flee together! I'll abandon my men. Just one word! Say one word!

KITTY: No! Flee alone! I want to die! I want them to kill me, since you won't do it. Beware! Time is running out. They're going to come; they're looking for you.

TOM BROWN: Up to the final moment I can escape and take you with me.

KITTY: Never!

TOM BROWN: I want your forgiveness! Listen to me, and if after what I'm going to tell you, you don't stretch your hand to me and tell me you forgive me, well, so be it! I'll kill you and myself afterwards.

KITTY: Speak. But you're wasting your time.

(*At this moment, Betty Blackthorn can be seen rising from the ground beneath the bridge.*)

BETTY BLACKTHORN (*low*): Ah, there he is!

TOM BROWN: I never knew either my father or my mother. I'm a stolen child too!

BETTY BLACKTHORN (*low*): He's not alone.

TOM BROWN: At two, some mountebanks stole me from my mother whose name I didn't learn until I was fifteen.

KITTY: I repeat: you're wasting your time and you won't soften my heart with your stories.

BETTY BLACKTHORN (*low*): Kitty's with him. I've got 'em both together. The two hates of my life .

TOM BROWN: These men taught me to live like them; to steal, because, in this world, they told me, some men have too much and others too little. They demonstrated that society was ill-balanced. That God, creating man, had given him the Earth and that those who had bought it up were the worst thieves, and those without were dupes. One day, they informed me that I was not the son of the wretched woman that, until that moment, I had been calling my mother.

BETTY BLACKTHORN (*low*): And the others haven't got here.

TOM BROWN: They said to me: Your real mother still lives. Wasn't that amusing! For me, who had never felt anything move me, that word "mother" went straight to my heart. I wanted to see her. I rushed to the village they'd mentioned to me, but she had vanished long ago.

BETTY BLACKTHORN (*low*): Ah, I hear them. They're coming at last.

TOM BROWN: I set about tearing it apart. I wanted to force them to reveal her. I ran through town and city. And everywhere, the name I uttered was unknown.

KITTY: That name... What was it?

TOM BROWN: Victoria Trevor!

BETTY BLACKTHORN (*after uttering a terrible scream*) Ah. Victoria Trevor! You said, Victoria Trevor!

TOM BROWN: Betty Blackthorn?

BETTY BLACKTHORN: And that's me! I'm Victoria Trevor! I'm the one who gave him up. Ah, God! God Almighty!

TOM BROWN: What are you doing here?

BETTY BLACKTHORN: I… I came to find you, so they could hang you. Because I'm with the police! Because I'm the one who gave you up!

TOM BROWN: You! Ah, miserable woman.

(*He rushes toward her.*)

BETTY BLACKTHORN (*screaming*): Don't kill me, you wretch! I am your mother! (*falling to her knees*)

TOM BROWN (*recoiling*): You? My mother!

BETTY BLACKTHORN (*struggling to her feet*): Yes, I am Victoria Trevor. Flee! Don't allow me to have remorse for having led you to the rope! Run away, will you! They're coming! They're a hundred paces off. I can hear them!

TOM BROWN (*repeating to himself*): My mother! My mother!

BETTY BLACKTHORN: Save yourself, will you, wretch!

TOM BROWN (*raising his head*): No! I won't. Not if Kitty won't come with me

BETTY BLACKTHORN: Kitty! I beg you! Save him! Don't let it be to me that he owes his death. That would be too horrible!

TOM BROWN: Kitty?

KITTY: Then, so be it! Go! I'll join you soon.

TOM BROWN: You swear to me?

KITTY: I swear to you.

TOM BROWN (*to his men in hiding*): Help me, the rest of you.

(*They run to him.*)

TOM BROWN: We are surrounded! Go through here! (*opening the gate to the sewer*) Get in there will you! You can hear them coming.

(*They all leave*.)

BETTY BLACKTHORN: Tom Brown! Gimme one kiss! Just one!

TOM BROWN (*kissing Betty*): Goodbye, mother. Till soon, Kitty!

(*He disappears into the mouth of the sewer and locks the gate behind him*.)

BETTY BLACKTHORN: My God! Please save him!

(*Inspector Lestrade enters from the right with his men, bearing torches. Nick Carter enters from the left*.)

INSPECTOR LESTRADE: Over this way! Ah! Betty! Where are they?

BETTY BLACKTHORN (*as if distracted*): Who?

INSPECTOR LESTRADE: Those you are giving up to us! Jack the Ripper and his gang.

BETTY BLACKTHORN: I don't know.

INSPECTOR LESTRADE: What do you mean, you don't know?

BETTY BLACKTHORN: I haven't seen them.

(*Mr. Robinson arrives from the bridge, followed by Sir William Huxley; they come down the steps.*)

ROBINSON: She's lying, Inspector. I saw them from the distance. They were talking with him.

KITTY: My God!

ROBINSON: They got away through there. (*pointing to the sewer gate*)

INSPECTOR LESTRADE (*rushing to it*): It's locked! Ah, the bandits, they're escaping! (*to his men*) Fire! Fire on them!

(*The police begin firing through the sewer grill. At the same moment, Betty rushes forward to shield her son and receives the discharge of the revolvers.*)

BETTY BLACKTHORN: Ah! (*She falls by the gate.*)

INSPECTOR LESTRADE: Wretched woman!

(*Inspector Lestrade pulls her from the gate. She rolls to the middle of the stage.*)

BETTY BLACKTHORN: At least, I die for him! (*she dies*)

(*Kitty faints in the arms of Sir William.*)

CURTAIN

# *ACT V*

## *SCENE VII*

A room in Sir James Plack's home. To the right, there is a fireplace with a clock on the mantelpiece; there are several lamps, lit. At the back, to the left, we see a portrait of a woman. The main door is to the rear. There are other doors to the left and right. In a cutaway, at the left, there is a window opening onto a terrace. Also, to the left, there is a telephone. Curtains, furniture, etc.

(*Toby enters furtively through the door at the back.*)

TOBY: I've managed to give the slip to that fat Mr. Robison... I saw a telephone over here. Ah, there it is. (*goes to the phone and presses the call button*) The Devil! If they ring back, it'll to make the Devil of a noise and bring the whole brood into Sir James' salon. I'm going to deaden it. (*placing his kerchief between the bell and the hammer of the ringer*) This way, the little chatterbox is muzzled. (*the ring of the response can be heard but it is muffled*) Hello! Communication with Lord Bradbury at the Grand Cafe Monaco in Tichborne Street. (*to himself looking at the clock*) Tom Brown is always there and all the waiters know him under the name Lord Bradbury. (*ringing*) Hello! To whom am I speaking? (*after having listened*) Ah, it's you! At last! I'm being held prisoner at Sir James Plack's. During the day, I was questioned by

Inspector Lestrade. I said nothing, of course. He wanted to take me to Scotland Yard, but at the request of that idiot, Robinson, who's taken it upon himself to get me to talk, they left me here. Come tonight with the others. There's a superb job to be done. There are only three men in the house, one is very ill, that's Sir James. I'm waiting for you. Hurry up! I'm getting moldy. (*listening*) Good! Around midnight then. (*hangs up the telephone*)

(*Mr. Robinson enters from the rear.*)

ROBINSON (*seeing Toby*): What are you doing here, you rascal?

TOBY: Me? I'm strolling around, taking the air.

ROBINSON: Where have you seen prisoners strolling around?

TOBY: Here, when the guards are asleep.

ROBINSON: It's true. Expecting you to sleep, I went to sleep as well. You have more fluid than I do, villain. (*looking around*) You haven't stolen anything?

TOBY: Oh, Mr. Robinson, for what do you take me?

ROBINSON: For a thief.

TOBY: What a bad opinion you have of me.

ROBINSON: If you want me to have a good one, tell me the place where the gang you belong to will meet.

TOBY: Why, I'm not part of any gang, Mr. Robinson! I'm the son of a merchant. And a merchant myself.

ROBINSON: You, a merchant!

TOBY: The house of Toby Jefferson and Company is famous.

ROBINSON: Famous? For what? Among thieves!

TOBY: Don't insult thieves, Mr. Robinson. It's thieves who provide a living for the police. If there were no thieves, there'd be no need for police. Then, what would the twenty thousand policeman who support the city of London do? Why, they'd become thieves! And it might be the actual thieves that would then be hired to become policemen. The world is but a come and go, Mr. Robinson. Today, I am the thief, and you the honest man. Tomorrow may come when I am rich and you are reduced to beggary, and tomorrow, I will be the honest man and you will be the thief.

ROBINSON: This scamp has strange but amusing theories.

TOBY: Theories of a thinker! Theories of a young man who understands politics. That's the social question. The true one. Time is money!

ROBINSON: I've never conceived the social question from that point of view.

(*Sir William Huxley enters from the left.*)

SIR WILLIAM HUXLEY: What are you doing here, Mr. Robinson?

ROBINSON: I was having a chat with this young philosopher, Sir William. Because it's not a vulgar thief we're dealing with; he's an orator of the true order, who, if he joins Parliament, will bring novel social theories to it, which will certainly stupefy his constituents. (*changing his tone*) How's Sir James doing?

SIR WILLIAM HUXLEY: Better. The doctor has triumphed over his shocking crisis. And what about that young girl?

ROBINSON: Miss Ellen is with her.

(*Ellen Plack enters from the right.*)

ELLEN PLACK: Nothing. I can't get anything from her. (*seeing Sir William*) Ah, it's you, my friend.

SIR WILLIAM HUXLEY: Will you please leave me alone for a moment with Miss Ellen, Mr. Robinson?

ROBINSON: Gladly! (*to Toby*) Come along, you!

TOBY: With pleasure, Mr. Robinson. (*aside*) At midnight, you won't be talking to me like that.

(*They leave by the back.*)

ELLEN PLACK: How is my father?

SIR WILLIAM HUXLEY: He's out of danger. A great calm has succeeded this feverish agitation which made us fear for him.

ELLEN PLACK: Ah, William, what don't I owe you! It's you who, through your assiduous cares, through the promptness with which you called for help, who's given me my father back! I loved you with all the strength of my heart before but now my life is yours!

SIR WILLIAM HUXLEY: Ellen, I want to do yet more. I hope to return joy to your family.

ELLEN PLACK: What do you mean?

SIR WILLIAM HUXLEY: I mean that I do not believe in Clary's death. I'm saying that this young girl deceived us by saying that Clary was dead.

ELLEN PLACK: My God!

SIR WILLIAM HUXLEY: I will make her tell the truth. I swear to you, I have an intuition…

ELLEN PLACK: Get to the point.

SIR WILLIAM HUXLEY: No! I can't tell you what I'm thinking.

(*Sir James Plack enters from the left.*)

SIR JAMES PLACK: Where is she? I want to see her! Where is she?

ELLEN PLACK (*rushing to him*): Father!

SIR JAMES PLACK (*sitting on a sofa*): Ah, it's you, my Ellen! My adored daughter! Oh, don't be afraid! It's over, quite over! If I was going to die of sorrow, I'd be dead by now. I have no right to die. Don't I have you? And aren't you my life?

ELLEN PLACK: Calm down, papa!

SIR JAMES PLACK: I am calm! Sir William told me that that young girl was here! You wanted to keep her around? That's fine! Very fine, child! She received the last kiss of our poor Clary, her last words. It seems to me it's she I am seeing again, and I want to place my lips where those of our beloved deceased were placed. Go find Kitty for me.

ELLEN PLACK: My kind father. Aren't you afraid that too much emotion…?

SIR JAMES PLACK: Go fetch me that young girl!

SIR WILLIAM HUXLEY (*low to Ellen*): Do as he says. It will serve my plans.

(*Ellen leaves.*)

SIR WILLIAM HUXLEY: If I may inquire, what do you plan to ask her, Sir James?

SIR JAMES PLACK: How she knew Clary, where she knew her, what my daughter died of. What do I know? I want her to talk to me about her, that's all.

(*Ellen returns with Kitty in tow.*)

KITTY (*to Ellen*): Ah, Miss, how kind you are!

ELLEN PLACK: My father is going to tell you that henceforth you are not to leave us.

KITTY (*moved*): Your father…

SIR JAMES PLACK (*still seated*): Come closer, child…

KITTY: They told me you were very ill, sir.

SIR JAMES PLACK: I almost died, it seems.

SIR WILLIAM HUXLEY: You see, Kitty, I wasn't lying to you.

SIR JAMES PLACK: Since I expatriated myself, since I left England, I've had only one thought, to return and find the little girl who was stolen from me. And, behold, at the moment when I really believed I had reached the goal of a lifetime of sufferings and anguish, I saw the collapse of all my hopes, the total annihilation of my dearest wishes. In the end, awful, meaningless death has come to separate me forever from the one I loved so much. (*to Ellen*) Don't be jealous, Ellen. You don't have the right to be jealous of the dead.

ELLEN PLACK: Father!

KITTY (*to herself*): No! No! I won't say a thing. His suffering would be much greater if he saw me as I am!

SIR JAMES PLACK: Kitty, tell me, where did you meet my Clary?

KITTY (*embarrassed*): At the dress maker where I learned to work.

SIR WILLIAM HUXLEY: Who placed her there?

KITTY: I don't know.

SIR WILLIAM HUXLEY: She never told you what she knew of her childhood?

KITTY: No!

SIR WILLIAM HUXLEY: What was the name of this dressmaker?

KITTY: I… I don't remember.

SIR WILLIAM HUXLEY: That's very singular! One doesn't forget so easily the names of persons who employed you…

ELLEN PLACK: Where is she located? (*silence*) I am asking you where she lived.

KITTY (*aside*): Will this torture never end?

SIR JAMES PLACK: Are you refusing to answer my daughter?

KITTY: It… It wasn't in London that we met.

SIR WILLIAM HUXLEY: In that case, where?

KITTY: In Bristol

SIR JAMES PLACK: Ah!

SIR WILLIAM HUXLEY (*staring at her*): Are you really telling us the truth?

KITTY (*weakly*): Yes.

SIR WILLIAM HUXLEY: Kitty, look at this portrait. (*pointing to it*) It's of Mrs. James Plack, the mother of Miss Ellen and Clary?

KITTY (*very moved*): She! She! Clary's mother!

SIR JAMES PLACK: What's wrong with you?

KITTY (*controlling herself*): Me? Nothing!

SIR WILLIAM HUXLEY: You appear very upset suddenly?

KITTY: Why should I be upset? I didn't know that lady. She's indifferent to me. I can only love her, because… because she used to love poor Clary.

SIR JAMES PLACK: She loved her so much that she died of despair.

KITTY: Of despair!

SIR WILLIAM HUXLEY (*pointing to the portrait*): Swear to me, swear to us, on the portrait of this venerated departed that you are really telling us the truth!

KITTY: My God!

SIR WILLIAM HUXLEY: Swear to us on the memory of she whose eyes are looking at you right now that you received the last kiss of her dying daughter.

KITTY: But why are you exacting this oath? Why don't you believe me? What interest would I have to lie?

SIR JAMES PLACK: I don't know, but Sir William is right. Swear!

KITTY (*after a moment*): I swear that Clary is dead! I swear it! I swear it!

(*A pause.*)

SIR WILLIAM HUXLEY: It seems I was mistaken

SIR JAMES PLACK: That's fine! That's all I wanted to know. You can go back to your room, child. (*dejectedly*) I am very unlucky.

KITTY (*aside*): They say that God pardons sins in proportion to what one suffers on Earth. Oh, I will be greatly forgiven then!

(*She leaves. Sir William takes his hat from a chair at the back.*)

SIR WILLIAM HUXLEY: I'm leaving too. Till tomorrow, Sir James (*shaking his hand*) Till tomorrow, Miss Ellen.

ELLEN PLACK (*accompanying him*): Till tomorrow, my dearest friend.

SIR WILLIAM HUXLEY: I'm going to see Inspector Lestrade. After talking to him, I'll return and pass by here.

ELLEN PLACK: Why?

SIR WILLIAM HUXLEY: To be near you.

ELLEN: How sweet. Till tomorrow

(*She shakes his hand and holds it for a minute, then he leaves. Sir James stands up.*)

SIR JAMES PLACK: Forgive me again, my dear Ellen, for the affection I have for the poor deceased.

ELLEN PLACK: Father, the dead have more right than the living to the tears of those who love them.

(*They leave. After a pause, the door at the right opens. Kitty slowly reenters, her eyes fixed on the portrait. She kneels before it.*)

KITTY (*arms extended to the portrait*): Mother! My dear mother! Please forgive me! I swore on your memory and I lied! Can I bear the same name as that pure and beautiful young girl? Can I receive the kisses of my father? Wouldn't it be a greater despair for them to see me living as I am, than to think me dead as they believe? Everything is forgotten, even death. Living, they would always have to blush for me. Forgive me! Forgive me! (*she bursts into sobs, her head in her hands*)

(*Ellen suddenly returns and places herself in front of Kitty.*)

ELLEN PLACK: Kitty! What are you doing?

KITTY (*standing up hastily*): My God!

ELLEN PLACK: By what right are you kneeling before the portrait of my mother?

KITTY: I never knew mine. They say that mothers who leave children on Earth will be reunited in Heaven. I thought that by praying before your mother, I was praying to mine.

ELLEN PLACK (*aside*): Ah! (*a long pause, then taking Kitty's hand*) In that case, let's pray.

(*They fall slowly to their knees.*)

ELLEN PLACK (*eyes fixed on Kitty*): Mother, bless your children! (*a pause*) Say it with me.

KITTY (*trembling*): Mother, bless your children!

ELLEN PLACK: Mother, reunite two sisters in your prayers to God!

KITTY (*rising excitedly*): What do you mean ?

ELLEN PLACK (*no longer able to control herself*): I mean that you are Clary!

KITTY: No!

ELLEN PLACK: Ah, I recognize you!

KITTY: No, no I tell you!

ELLEN PLACK: I don't know what incomprehensible motive makes you push us away, but you won't deceive me anymore! You *are* Clary. You *are* my sister! And I am waiting for you in my arms!

KITTY (*at the end of her strength*): Ah, Ellen, Ellen!

(*She throws herself into Ellen's arms, weeping.*)

ELLEN PLACK: But what was it that kept you from embracing us?

KITTY (*after a silence*): Shame!

ELLEN PLACK: Shame?

KITTY: Ellen, I was wrong to confess to you! Run away from me! Don't come near me. I will soil you. I haven't had the strength to shut up! Yes, I am Clary, but keep this secret. Don't ever tell our father! Ah, I beg you, I entreat you!

ELLEN PLACK: You must be mad!

KITTY: Ellen! Please!

ELLEN PLACK: You forbid me to come near you? Is it up to me to judge you? You are my sister and I love you.

(*She entwines Kitty and covers her with kisses.*)

KITTY (*in her arms*): Ah, how happy I am!

(*Suddenly, Ellen pulls away and goes to the door at the right.*)

KITTY: Where are you going?

ELLEN PLACK: Why, to our father, he'll be so happy…

KITTY: No! Oh, no! Don't do that! Don't you understand? He'll die of shame if he knows what I am!

ELLEN PLACK: He'll love you whatever you may be, whatever you have been. He'll love you!

KITTY: Ah, God! You are pitiless, Ellen. Take me away! He might come here and I don't want it. No, I don't want to appear before him yet.

ELLEN PLACK: Come! Come on, will you!

KITTY: Ah, God! Death now! Make me die!

(*They leave. Toby enters at the back.*)

TOBY: That fat pig's snoozing again. Let's see if the comrades have gotten here… (*going to open a window*) How dark it is out there! (*making a bird noise*) Hoot! Hoot! (*the signal is repeated outside*) That's Tom Brown! Ah, I see someone moving in the shadows. They've placed a ladder against the wall. Great! Nothing to fear! Climb up, boys!

(*Tom Brown enters through the window.*)

TOM BROWN: Thanks, Toby.

TOBY: Think nothing of it, boss. How many are you?

TOM BROWN: Six, counting you and me. Two will come at the first call, and two others will watch.

TOBY: Good.

TOM BROWN: Where's Sir James' room?

TOBY (*indicating*): At the end of that corridor. And it's a long one. (*pointing to the right*) First door on the right is Miss Ellen's.

TOM BROWN: Beautiful! Go fetch me Sir James!

TOBY: On my way…

(*Suddenly, Sir James returns unexpectedly.*)

TOBY: Talk about the Devil! Here he is. (*goes to the window*)

SIR JAMES PLACK (*to Tom Brown*): Who are you? What are you doing in my home at this hour?

TOM BROWN: Who am I? It matters little to you. You don't know me. Simply imagine that I am a thief, and that I've come to ask 20,000 pounds of you.

SIR JAMES PLACK: A thief?

TOM BROWN: I will add that this home is isolated and no one will come if you shout (*gesturing to Toby*)

(*Toby gestures to Bartlett and Topps outside, who climb through the window into the room.*)

TOM BROWN: So, if in two minutes, you haven't given me the 20,000 pounds which I am asking for, these two honest lads (*pointing*), my associates, that I have the honor of introducing to you, will carry off your daughter, Miss Ellen, to a safe place known only to me.

SIR JAMES PLACK: Ah! Bandits!

TOM BROWN: Insults! (*to his men*) Go!

TOBY: Follow me.

(*They go out.*)

SIR JAMES PLACK: Oh! But I will defend her!

TOM BROWN (revolver in hand): I don't think so!

(*Ellen appears, dragged into the room by the bandits.*)

ELLEN PLACK: Father! Help!

TOM BROWN: Don't be afraid, Miss. As soon as your father counts us out the 20,000 pounds that I've requested of him, you will be free.

ELLEN PLACK (*struggling*): Father! Father!

TOM BROWN: Miss Plack, if you continue to scream, I swear to you that I will kill Sir James. (*aiming at him*)

(*Kitty enters and rushes to Sir James' side*.)

KITTY: Ah, no, you won't do that!

TOM BROWN: Kitty!?

KITTY: You won't kill my father!

SIR JAMES PLACK: Ah!

(*He crushes her in his arms*.)

TOM BROWN: Your father?

KITTY: He would have killed you, that swine!

TOM BROWN (*with rage*): Kitty!

KITTY: He's a murderous coward, too!

TOM BROWN: Kitty, take care!

KITTY: Of what? Of death? Why, free me then, of this life that I abhor!

TOM BROWN: Yes, I'm going to kill you!

(*Mr. Robinson, holding a revolver, enters from the left.*)

ROBINSON: Not yet!

(*He fires on Tom Brown, who falls.*)

BARTLETT: Run away!.

(*The bandits all rush toward the window. Nick Carter appears suddenly, revolver in hand.*)

NICK CARTER: Stop there!

TOPPS: Nabbed!

TOBY: This way!

(*They run toward the back. Inspector Lestrade appears surrounded by detectives.*)

INSPECTOR LESTRADE: In the name of the Queen, I arrest you! Seize these scoundrels.

(*The detectives surround the bandits.*)

SIR JAMES: PLACK My daughter, my daughter! (*he presses Kitty into his arms*)

KITTY: I'm ashamed. This is Ellen's place.

SIR JAMES PLACK: Next to you.

INSPECTOR LESTRADE: The accomplices?

NICK CARTER: They've escaped.

TOM BROWN (*rising up*): Escaped! Ah, Jack the Ripper's going to die, but Jack the Ripper is not dead! Others will rise up to avenge those hanged at Newgate. (*to Kitty*) Kitty, Kitty!

KITTY (*with horror*): Ah, shut-up! I hate you now!

TOM BROWN: You hate me? In that case, I'm glad to die!

(He dies.)

ROBINSON: And I've saved England. Again.

INSPECTOR LESTRADE: What do you mean, "Again?"

(*Mr. Robinson begins removing his disguise.*)

ROBINSON: Come on, Lestrade!

INSPECTOR LESTRADE: What are you doing?

ROBINSON : Ridding myself of this ridiculous disguise.

INSPECTOR LESTRADE (*recognizing him*): Sherlock Holmes!

ALL: Sherlock Holmes!

SHERLOCK HOLMES: As you see.

INSPECTOR LESTRADE (*furious*): Not again!

SHERLOCK HOLMES: I told you I'd begun my investigation, Lestrade. Maybe next time you'll listen.

CURTAIN

# The Secret Files of the King of Detectives: JACK THE RIPPER (1908)

## *I. The Detectives' Bet*

"It's an affair that seizes me by the throat, Mr. Holmes—and I've come to you as a last resource. I don't see any other way to solve a mystery which is becoming more frightful every day."

It was with these words that Mr. Warren, Chief of the London Police, received the famous detective who had just entered his office.

"I'm back from Italy," said Sherlock Holmes, "where I was lucky enough to succeed in a very delicate matter. I found your letter, sir. I saw you had an urgent communication to make to me, and here I am."

The two men shook hands. They then sat down comfortably in two leather armchair near a small table.

"Was your stay in Italy long?" asked the Chief of Police.

"About three months."

"Despite that, you must have heard of the scourge which has fallen on London? The newspapers must have informed you that the Police are on burning coals."

"Ah, you are speaking of Jack the Ripper?"

"Naturally, and all of London, Europe, the world even, will speak to you of him, just as I do. For centuries, I can testify, there hasn't been a comparable mystery to that which this mysterious individual poses to us. I assure you, Mr. Holmes, that there are moments when I think of rendering my resignation into the hands of Her Gracious Majesty, who will no doubt entrust my job to someone younger and more capable than myself, just to no longer have this vision from beyond the grave always present before my eyes."

"From beyond the grave?" smiled the detective. "I think on the contrary that we are dealing with a man of flesh and blood, and I don't see why it should be difficult to end the exploits of this person."

"What a consolation to hear such words in a mouth like yours, Mr. Holmes" said Mr. Warren, slowly regaining his confidence. "Have a cigar—and light it up, will you? Our conversation is going to last for a while, and I've given orders that we are not to be disturbed under any pretext."

And the Chief of Police presented the Detective with a small ivory box filled with excellent, imported cigars. Holmes took one, cut it and lit it. The Police Officer followed his example.

An odorous blue smoke invaded the office where these two men, true luminaries in the field of criminal investigation, were going to decide in some way the future fate of London.

"You've learned from the newspapers all that concerns Jack the Ripper. For that reason, I'm going to get to the point quickly, and limit myself to the bare bones of the problem.

"Three months ago, at the main police station, we came across a case that initially didn't disturb us too much. A murder had been committed in Whitechapel, in Gloucester Street, one of the most ill famed in that neighborhood, under a carriage entrance. A young woman—a prostitute as it was discovered later—was found with her belly slit open, atrociously mutilated.

"Mr. Hunter, the Superintendent in charge of Whitechapel, was called. He concluded that it was a crime of passion. As you know, there are criminals who feel compelled to kill the woman they've just taken. It's a sick passion, the work of a lunatic, something that is more the concern of Bedlam Asylum than that of the Scotland Yard…"

"Bravo! I share your just and humanitarian opinion, Mr. Warren," replied Sherlock Holmes.

"The murder of Gloucester Street nevertheless remained obscure," continued the Chief of Police. "Our inquiries eventually concluded that a suspect had indeed been spotted in the street, but no one was able to provide us with a good description. According to some, he wore a yellow overcoat; but for others, he had no overcoat. A sailor swore great oaths that the suspect wore a beard. To the contrary, the proprietor of a neighboring bar maintained that he was beardless.

"The girl was buried. The case was closed. Three days later, another murder happened, on Greenwich Road. This time, it was the wife of a sailor. Her husband was still in India. A young and pretty girl, my word! She was walking home late from a friend's house and was killed in the same manner."

"It's the verification of the theory of the repetition of facts," said Holmes, smiling. "You know that we criminalists believe, as do doctors, that any remarkable case will reoccur, the same day or shortly thereafter, under identical conditions."

"Well, in this case, the theory has been abundantly verified," continued Warren. "One crime followed another. In one week, eight young women were the victim of the same, mysterious killer. Always the same kind of death. The victims were attacked and murdered in the street, dragged under a carriage entrance, to a stable or a courtyard, in short, a place where the murderer was certain not to be interrupted for the few moments necessary to complete his grisly task.

"Then with a well-sharpened knife, the killed slit their womb open in a manner that I could only characterize as skilled—and death soon followed."

"None of these unfortunate victims was able to make a declaration before dying?"

"None. In every case, death had occurred before the arrival of the police or the public. Soon, it became evident that the murderer was not content with just the wretched prostitutes and women of loose morals whom he met in Whitechapel and neighboring areas usually frequented by prostitutes. Several women and young girls of excellent families have also become his prey. However, I must share with you a conclusion that we reached after the most thorough inquiry by our best detectives: all these women led a secret, double life. Remember that, Mr. Holmes, it must be important."

"Actually, I share your opinion," replied the Detective. "And how many murders have there been in total?"

"Up to now, in three months' time, thirty-seven women have been murdered in this manner. A panic has spread throughout the entire city. No woman, no young girl, dares to go out at night anymore, even accompanied.

"Popular voice has given a name to the murderer; they call him Jack the Ripper. As far as we're concerned, we haven't been spared reproaches. The newspapers rant daily against us, and challenge us to put an end to these crimes. My masters have formally instructed me to capture Jack the Ripper at all costs, but I just don't see how!

"Tell me, Mr. Holmes, you who are the best criminal investigator in the world, how could you stop a man who hides in the shadows like a ghost, who commits his crimes in minutes, and vanish afterwards without leaving a trace, a man who always operates in the same manner, but manifests himself ceaselessly throughout the city, and seems to be in league with the Devil himself? For no one ever got there in time to hear the victims' cries of agony, nor to see the murderer get away..."

Sherlock Holmes rubbed his recently shaved chin with his hand.

"Would you allow me to ask you a few questions, Mr. Warren?"

"What do you think, Mr. Holmes? I beg you to! I will answer you to the best of my abilities."

The Detective puffed a few smoke rings out from his cigar. He looked pensively at them and seemed to find some pleasure in that sight.

"You said just now," he then remarked, "that the murderer always operates in the same manner. Have your doctors determined if he always uses the same instrument, the same knife?"

"I can reply unambiguously 'yes.' We have consulted the most illustrious doctors in London, and they have worked on the case with the greatest eagerness. Some of them claim that the murderer can only be a butcher or a butcher's apprentice. Others actually say that he might be a surgeon. The victims' wombs were opened as if he'd performed a laparectomy."

"Did the bodies have any parts missing, or were they intact?"

"They were intact, but in many instances, the intestines had been pulled out."

"Was there any theft accompanying the crime, in at least one case?"

"No, not one. In the last case, a murder committed in Montgomery Street, the victim was the wife of a rich merchant. She had a wallet containing 20,000 pounds on her. Not one note was missing. And all her jewels were there."

"Naturally, you've positioned an army of detectives to try to catch Jack the Ripper *in flagrante delicto*?"

"Of course! You must realize, Mr. Holmes, that all my men are burning with desire to distinguish themselves in this affair. They've spent whole nights laying traps. Our entire force has been mobilized. We've organized signals. We've provided all the street walkers of London with a special whistle. If they're attacked, they only have to use it..."

"And have they?"

"Never," replied Mr. Warren. "And yet, some of the victims had the whistle in their pocket, or hanging around their necks. I've also promised a reward for the arrest of Jack the Ripper—a considerable sum, a thousand pounds. I hoped that we'd find a snitch, a man familiar with his crimes, who would want to earn his blood money by turning him in. But no one has yet presented himself with any reliable clue..."

At this moment, there was a rap on the door.

"Who's that?" asked the Chief of Police, visibly vexed. "Didn't I expressly leave orders that I was not to be disturbed as long as Mr. Holmes was here?"

A man entered and bowed respectfully.

"Ah, it's you, Lestrade," said Mr. Warren in a softened voice. "Doubtless, you're bringing me some important news? To interrupt my conference with Mr. Holmes, it must be a question of great importance."

"It is, sir. Very bad news—the thirty-eighth case has just landed on my desk."

"What! The Ripper has struck again?"

"With one major difference, sir. This time, the victim is a celebrity. It will cause an enormous scandal. The singer Lillian Bell was murdered tonight."

"Lillian Bell," repeated the Chief of Police, "admired by all—who's performed before the Queen herself… It's not possible."

"From what we were able to determine so far, sir," continued the Inspector, "the singer had performed yesterday in Drury Lane with her customary success. Afterwards, she changed in her dressing room, and left the theatre with her dresser to take a carriage that was waiting to carry her to her lodgings in Oxford Street. The dresser usually accompanied her to the carriage. Yet, last night, Miss Bell left her at the stage door for some unknown reason and went to the carriage by herself. When the coach reached her residence, he was surprised to not see her come out of the cab. When he opened the door, he found Miss Bell lying on silk cushions savagely mutilated. The police was called and concluded it was yet another of Jack the Ripper's murders."

"This is truly awful," said Warren, mopping his face with a kerchief. "We can expect a severe trouncing from the Press."

"I'm convinced that, yet again, we're going to be groping in the dark. This crime seems to be even more mysterious than the other thirty-seven," said Lestrade.

"I agree with the Inspector," said Holmes, "it's very mysterious and complicated indeed. But I'm certain Mr.

Lestrade will doubtless shed light on it. I wish you good luck."

"Don't joke, Mr. Holmes," replied Lestrade, venomously. "Try to find Jack yourself amongst the city's five million inhabitants. It's like searching for a needle in a haystack!"

"But I will find him, my friend. In fact, may I suggest a little bet, that is, if you feel brave enough?"

"Brave? I'm brave enough to go to Hell itself and back if need be."

"Very good!" said Holmes, offering his hand. "I know that you've often suggested in the past that I owed my successes to pure luck only."

"That is so," replied Lestrade.

"Then, let's bet on who's going to be the first to catch Jack the Ripper: you or I."

"I'll take that bet," said Lestrade.

"A true detective's bet," said Mr. Warren, rubbing his hands in glee. "I'll be your witness and set the bet at twenty-five bottles of French champagne that we will drink together the day Jack the Ripper has been arrested. Now, let the best man win!"

The two detectives shook hands.

"And now," said Holmes, "I must leave you as I don't have a moment to lose. As of now, I am officially in pursuit of Jack the Ripper."

## *II. The Mysterious Undertaker*

Because of her fame, the corpse of Lillian Bell had not been taken to the Morgue but lay in her bed in her home. Next to it were flowers in abundance, two tall candelabra and a cross. It was a sad spectacle: that of the flower of youth mowed down by an insatiable Death.

Two people stood next to the bed. One was a thin blond young man with dissipated features indicative of a dissolute lifestyle. He was dressed smartly, if even a little eccentrically. The other was a pretty young woman of 23, Miss Harriet Blunt, Lillian Bell's chamber-maid, born into a good family. She had been the late singer's right hand and confidante.

"What a terrible event," said the young man, staring at his gloved hands. "I still feel the terror I felt when I first heard the news. I was having breakfast at my club and threw myself into a cab to come here right away. My poor sister! Who would have expected such a terrible end?"

Harriet wept."If only I had been with her, this horrible event might not have taken place. I had asked Miss Lillian the permission to go out for half-an-hour to take care of some pressing private matter. She was so kind that she hadn't insisted I stay with her."

"Perhaps your presence would not have prevented her murder. Indeed, you should be grateful you weren't in that cab with her, otherwise you yourself might be lying here beside her, another victim of that monstrous Jack the Ripper."

Miss Harriet shivered.

"I have a question for you, Miss Harriet—in the strictest confidence, of course… You were my sister's closest companion. Did she leave a large fortune? By my estimate, I think she must have amassed at least 100,000 pounds..."

"Something like that, yes. The money is in an account with the Bank of England."

"And naturally, she left a will? I must be her only heir. Of course, we had our share of squabbles in the past, but I know that deep down, she loved me deeply."

"She did indeed, Mr. Bell, but you gave her some serious reasons not to."

"You, too? Well, she insisted on complete freedom for herself, but wanted me to live the life of a petty clerk."

Suddenly, there was knock at the door.

"My God, who is this?" said Harriet, having ran to the door and opened it, revealing the impressive figure of a tall, gaunt man dressed all in black from head to toes. He had a pointy nose and slick black hair combed back on his skull.

"Don't be afraid, Miss Harriet," said Grover Bell. "I'm sure this gentleman will introduce himself and kindly explain the purpose of his visit."

"My name is Josiah Wakefield," said the man in black. "I represent the funeral home *Requiescat In Pace*. As soon as I learned of the sad event, which touched us deeply, I came to present to you, in the name of the funeral home, the expression of our profound sympathy, and, at the same time, to present you our prospectus. It explains all our fees and charges. We take care of everything."

"My good man," said Grover Bell, "I can't make a decision about my sister's funerals until the police investigation has been completed. Doubtless, the Coroner will want to examine the body, perhaps even order an autopsy."

"I thought so, of course, but perhaps you might allow me to take some measurements and preparations so that I need not return and disturb you further?"

"I see nothing wrong in that," said Grover Bell. "We'll go into the side room. Come, Miss Harriet, the gentleman won't need our help."

"I'll be quick," said Me. Wakefield, pulling out a tape measure from his pocket. "You can glance at our prospectus while I take the necessary measurements. Note that we are the largest funeral home in London..."

And he began making notes of the results in his notebook.

After the brother and the maid left, Wakefield suddenly lifted the shroud covering the body and exposed the wounds. He looked at them very carefully with an expert eye. Then, recovering the body, he examined the hands of the deceased which were adorned with several valuable rings. He paid particular attention to her pale fingernails.

"No evidence of a struggle," he muttered. "No broken fingernails, no bruises. Should I conclude that Lillian Bell knew her murderer? That she invited him inter her cap, not expecting an attack?... Ah-ha! What's this? A hair or some beard?" The undertaker pulled out a magnifying glass. "No, not a beard or hair, but from a wig or false beard. So, fact number one: Jack the Ripper wears a disguise when he commits his crimes. So, he is unlikely to be a brute, or a savage. He's an intelligent man, likely high on the social ladder, despite his abominable vice…"

The Undertaker then opened the singer's mouth. Her perfect dentition had been admired throughout England. At once, he made a discovery that, if known, would have caused a sensation in the press. "A false tooth! But very well made…" He carefully removed the tooth and examined it under his magnifying glass. "And unless I'm mistaken, this little gold ring which surrounds the rubber piece that held the tooth in place proves that Miss Bell had smoked opium. Interesting… Opium dens may have been Miss Bell's only connection with the underworld. This is where I'll begin my investigation!"

As the undertaker replaced the tooth, he dropped his magnifying glass which rolled under the bed. Stooping to pick it up hurriedly, he discovered someone already concealed beneath it!

"Come out, my friend," the undertaker said. "You're caught."

Despite his resistance, the person concealed beneath the bed was pulled out. He was dressed as a vagrant and wore a hirsute, red beard.

"I wasn't trying to steal anything," grumbled the man. He then pulled out a coin from his pocket. "There. Take this and say nothing."

"Do you think I can be bought?" replied the undertaker. "And so cheaply too! I want a pound for my silence!"

"You thief!" said the man, depositing more coins in the undertaker's hand. "There's a pound. Now, go away!"

The undertaker pocketed the money, then wrote something in his notebook, tore the page and gave it to the other man.

“What’s that?” he said, taking the piece of paper.

“Read it and you’ll find out.”

The man read: *Receipt for the sum of Ten Pounds from Inspector Lestrade as a Charitable Contribution to the Metropolitan Police Orphanage.*

“The Devil! You knew who I was!”said Lestrade, checking to see if his wig and false beard were still in place.

“Of course! I knew who you were from the moment I pulled you from under that bed. I know you have a bunion on your left toe, pressing against your shoe.”

“Holmes!” said Lestrade.

“I wish you good luck in your investigation. Thank you for kind contribution. Sorry to have disturbed you. You can go back under the bed now.”

And Sherlock Holmes left, laughing.

## *III. In the Opium Den*

The vice of opium use had been popular in the highest ranks of society in London for some time. Very distinguished men and women had become the prey of the opium demon, and slipped in secret to opium dens, sometimes without even bothering with a disguise.

Users were pale. They were the shadows of human beings, with blank, glistening eyes and withered faces. They were walking cadavers.

Once Holmes was certain that Lillian Bell had smoked opium, he hastened home to change his disguise. He hid his hair under a dark wig, and covered his face with white fat. This gave him a sickly appearance which he augmented with dark circles under his eyes. A drop of belladonna to his eyes gave him a feverish look which completed the picture of an opium addict.

"You look like a walking cadaver, or someone with an intense fever, Holmes," exclaimed Doctor Watson who had come at the detective's request to assist him in this important investigation.

"Thank you, Doctor. That's exactly the effect I desire. What you see is common to all opium users. Cheeks withered and wrinkled, eyes dazzling with an extraordinary fire."

"Yes, of course, the disguise is perfect. But what is the purpose of it? And where are you going under this disguise?"

"I've no time to explain. But I may need your assistance."

"Do you want me to accompany you?"

"No, I want you to stay here and be ready to assist me if I need your help. I won't return tonight," Holmes said, as he placed a revolver and dagger in his pocket, "so you mustn't follow me. Stay here. I'll wire you if I need you. Hush! I don't want Mrs. Hudson to see me like this."

Watson nodded.

Holmes left stealthily.

After leaving Baker Street, Holmes headed rapidly towards the Thames, crossed the bridge near Southwark Street and made his way to Tooly Street. There, he was confronted by a long row of houses that faced the Thames on one side and the South Eastern Railway on the other. Holmes finally arrived at a two-story house, undoubtedly dating from the time of Cromwell, but still managing to preserve a measure of shabby elegance.

Holmes knocked discreetly at the door, then rang. The door was opened by a black man dressed in Baroque livery.

"What do you want?"

"I want to speak to Madame Cajana."

The servant led him into an elegantly furnished room. There he saw a dark-skinned woman whose jet-black hair was graying around the temples. She was dressed in western clothes, but still managed to look very exotic.

"You wanna talk to me?" Madame Cajana drawled in a strongly-accented English. "Watcha want?"

"To smoke opium."

"An' who tole you, you could do that hiya? Sombody's kiddin' you?"

"You can see by looking at my face that I'm an addict to the sport."

She looked at his face very carefully before responding:

"You do look like a user. You are indeed of our sect. But, I gotta be careful. Very careful."

"I really need a fix. I've got to have it or I'll go crazy."

"Calm down. You'll get what you need here."

"How much?"

"Five pounds."

Holmes quickly offered the money.

Madame Cajana then led him to another room with couches and pipes.

"Would you prefer to serve yourself, sir? Or should I remain with you to fix the pipes?"

"I'd prefer that. I'm very emotional at the moment and I don't like being alone."

"Nothing could be easier. "

She began to prepare the pipe.

"First, as soon as the water boils…"

After quietly getting between her and the door, Holmes said in his natural, commanding voice:

"I know all that, Madame. I didn't come here to learn from you how to prepare an opium pipe."

She turned, frightened by the change of tone in his voice.

"Remain calm," said the detective. "If you call for help, you are ruined. I'll have you arrested immediately."

She froze and watched him warily.

"Who are you?"

"Sherlock Holmes."

"You!"

“Yes. Now answer my questions frankly, and I promise you not to betray the secret of your house. But do not attempt to deceive me.”

“What do you want to know?”

“Did the singer Lillian Bell frequent your house?” asked the detective.

“Why do you ask me that?” replied Madame Cajana. “You know that the first duty of the proprietor of an opium den is not to betray her clients.”

“You must in this case,” said Holmes in a firm voice. “She’s been murdered—by Jack the Ripper.”

“Murdered. By… by…”

“Yes.”

“All I know is that she was beginning to smoke seriously. But she didn’t come here often.”

“Who sent her to you?”

“She came at the recommendation of a man I must respect absolutely. You know that I must protect my clients. And I just don’t take anyone. You saw how suspicious I was with you when you came in.”

“True. Therefore I believe that the recommendation you mentioned must have carried a lot of weight. I must absolutely know that man’s name.”

Madame Cajana twisted her hands.

“Mr. Holmes, I beg you, please! I can offer you money… Five hundred pounds?”

“You’re wasting your time. Sherlock Holmes isn’t for sale. I repeat my question: who was that man?”

“It was an Indian Doctor.”

“An Indian Doctor? Someone from your country?”

“No,” said Madame Cajana, shaking her head. “He wasn’t born in India, but he’s lived there for a long time. He speaks the language better than I do.”

“Ah—an Englishman then?”

"Yes. A learned man. He's sent me many customers over the years."

"A funny doctor, who prescribes opium as if it were just another medicine. What's his name?"

"I swear to you, Mr. Holmes, I don't know his name. I've always heard him mentioned the 'Indian Doctor.' I never asked his name—just as I didn't ask yours. Besides, he doesn't come very often—and never smokes opium himself. He just sits here and watches…"

Suddenly, Madame Cajana stopped. They heard a noise from one of the adjacent rooms. Holmes recognized it as the muffled sound that addicts occasionally make when in throes to the delights of the drug.

"Who's in the next room?" asked the detective. It sounds like a woman…"

"Yes, but I don't know who she is. As I told you, I never ask for names."

"Perhaps, but don't tell me you don't employ spies to follow your clients and discover their names for blackmail."

"Blackmail! Never! I'm an honest woman!" protested Madame Cajana.

She spoke with conviction. As Holmes was about to make a further effort to pry information from her, there was a piercing scream. They both stared at the door of the room whence the scream had come.

"That scream!" said the detective. "I know it all too well! It's that of a person being murdered! Something awful is taking place right now in that room!"

Holmes rushed to the door, but found it locked.

"Quick! Let me in!" he shouted to Madame Cajana, as another scream sounded.

The Indian woman began pulling her keys out, but she was so flustered that she could not find the right one.

From behind the door, Holmes heard the sound of breaking glass. Impatiently, the detective broke down the door.

Entering the adjacent room, Holmes found the butchered body of a young woman. And a window broken open.

"Jack the Ripper was here."

Madame Cajana screamed and fainted.

## *IV. A Moving Train*

Holmes rushed to the window. The Ripper had broken the glass and escaped onto a gallery that surrounded the house. Holmes climbed through the window and onto the gallery.

Looking around, the detective saw a shape huddled against the wall in the moonlight. The shape moved slightly revealing a broad-shouldered man in a cape rather similar to Holmes'. He appeared to sport a long black beard.

"Surrender, Jack the Ripper! I arrest you!"

Holmes aimed his pistol directly at the monster.

But at this moment, a train whistle echoed and the red light of a fast moving express approached.

The Ripper eyed the train rapidly, calculating the distance he would have to leap.

"Don't jump or I'll shoot!" shouted the detective. "If I cannot take you alive, I'll take you dead!"

The only response was a mad ironic laugh. Holmes rushed toward him, but the Ripper leaped with incredible agility over the balustrade and landed on the top of a passing boxcar.

Holmes fired several times but missed.

"That was the act of a man damned, who dares anything. He's escaped me for now, but I've had a look at him, that may be useful…"

Abandoning hope of catching the Ripper, Holmes turned his attention to the scene of the crime, hoping that the murderer had left some clue that would reveal his identity or allow him to be traced.

He retraced his steps and stepped back through the shattered window. There, he found several servants milling about the body and Madame Cajana, who had now recovered from her faint

Holmes ordered the servants to leave, but gesturing for Madame Cajana to remain. Obediently, they did so. After they were alone, he began to examine the body. The victim was a young girl with curly, blond hair. Her face still reflected an expression of kindness that even her violent death had not succeeded in erasing. She was dressed in a frilly white shirt splattered with blood.

The detective's eyes also spotted a handkerchief with the initials "I" and "M" surmounted by a crown.

"Madame Cajana, do you know the deceased?" he asaked.

"No, I don't know her," replied the Indian woman, whining. "Ah! I'm lost! The police will come and arrest me now! All because of that awful murder! I swear to you, Mister Holmes…"

"Don't swear and tell me everything you know. Was this the first time she'd come to you?"

"No, it's the fourth or fifth time."

"Most recently?"

"Last month."

"Did she smoke opium? I noticed that her apparatus is cold."

"Each time she came, she stayed by herself. She didn't need assistance, nor did she want any."

"Did she always lock her door?"

"Yes, always. I have duplicates."

"And you never went in?"

"Never! What for? I just refilled the pipes. I supposed she smoked, but I never saw any visible proof of it."

Holmes walked back to the window, looked outside, especially at the gallery, and said:

"Madame Cajana, I am of the opinion that this young woman came here not to smoke, but to see someone she couldn't meet elsewhere."

"But we would have seen him."

"Not necessarily. A man could easily climb in through the window, using that outside gallery, which is easily accessible from the back street."

"But why would she give a rendez-vous to Jack the Ripper?"

"Good question. I think the Ripper knew she expected a nocturnal visitor here—and came instead."

"But why would he kill her?"

"Ah, that's another matter. Who knows what evil lurks in the hearts of some men… Now, Madame Cajana, show me where this unfortunate woman might have stored her outer garments and belongings."

Madame Cajana opened a closet. Holmes examined the clothes, but there was no personal identification. All that he could find was a jacket, again embroidered with the initials "I" and "M" surmounted by a crown.

"Unless I am greatly mistaken, this jacket belongs to a French Countess," Holmes mused.

The woman's purse contained only a few gold coins, a small mirror and some makeup, and another kerchief.

Her shoes were expensive and hand-made. After placing the shoes on the feet of the deceased to verify that they indeed belonged to the deceased, Holmes examined them and saw the manufacturer's stamp: they had been made by Laurin & Co., on Howard Street. Holmes decided he would pay them a visit, and pocketed the shoes.

"What must I do ?" asked Madame Cajana.

"Inform the Police! I'll take charge of that duty, but make sure not to touch or hide anything here."

Holmes quickly left and took a cab to Howard Street where a certain number of firms had recently chosen to remain open all night, more as a way of advertising than actually selling.

The cab left him at the entrance to Laurin & Co., a firm that proudly advertised itself as "makers of fine Parisian shoes." Late though it was, the showroom was brilliantly lit. An obviously French attendant came to welcome the new customer.

"Would you be kind enough to tell me if these shoes were made or sold by your firm?" asked the detective

"Certainly, sir."

After looking at the shoes carefully, and examining the quality, the attendant smiled proudly and confirmed that they were of the best workmanship and indeed were most likely sold by their firm.

"Do you recall the buyer?"

"That would be impossible, sir, as we sell so many shoes."

"These appear to have been made to measure, however."

"Why, you're right. In that case, perhaps, I can help you. We keep files."

He rang, and a young woman appeared.

"Mademoiselle Daisy," said the attendant, "do you recall by chance for whom these shoes were made?"

"Certainly. We rarely make shoes that small. They were made for the Comtesse Irene de Malmaison."

"Ah, a member of the French community in London," said the detective.

"Yes, sir. A most elegant lady, if I may say so."

"Do you have a record of her address?"

"Certainly, but we do not disclose such information about our clients…"

"I am Sherlock Holmes. The Comtesse has just been murdered by Jack the Ripper and I am trying to catch her assassin."

"*Mon Dieu!*"

Without further ado, the attendant gave Holmes all the information that he possessed.

## *V. A Hard-Hearted Father*

"Despite the lateness of the hour, Monsieur le Marquis will receive you. Be kind enough to follow me," said the butler, leading Holmes, now dressed in his usual manner, into a handsomely furnished library lit by a lamp with a green shade.

A few minutes later, the Marquis appeared, impeccably dressed.

"Are you the famous detective? I've heard a lot about you, Monsieur Holmes. Still, I am astonished that you've come to see me. To what do I owe the honor? "

"A tragic circumstance. A misfortune has befallen your daughter Irene."

"Irene? How can that be? She is in her room. She has a migraine, and refused to go to the Opera with me. You must be mistaken."

"In no way. I am very certain of my information. However, the simplest thing to do is to send for her."

The Marquis gestured to the same butler who had admitted Holmes. The servant bowed and left. After a few moments, he returned and said:

"Monsieur le Marquise, the Comtesse's chambermaid says that she is nowhere to be found."

"In that case, where is she? Ask the chambermaid to come here!"

"It's worse than you think, Monsieur le Marquis," interrupted Holmes. "Your daughter is dead."

"It's not possible. I saw her just a few hours ago—in perfect health."

"Your daughter was murdered."

Visibly shaken, the Marquis sank into a chair.

"Murdered? Now I understand why you're here, Mister Holmes. …And by whom?"

"By Jack the Ripper."

"Where was she, the poor child? Mister Holmes, if it wasn't you delivering this terrible news to me in person, I would believe I'm the victim of some kind of horrible joke—or someone is trying to drive me to despair. Where did this ghastly murder occur?"

"In an opium den located near the Thames and belonging to an Indian woman named Madame Cajana."

After a good deal of agitation, the Marquis mastered himself and asked coldly:

"An opium den… How did she get there?"

"She'd frequented the establishment several times in the last month. "

"My daughter frequented an opium den? In that case, my loss is not as great as I thought. Let's change the subject. You've done your duty, Mister Holmes, and I consider myself greatly obliged to you."

"Then, perhaps you will allow me to examine the Comtesse's boudoir? I hope to find something there that will put me on the scent of her murderer."

"Everything is at your disposal, Monsieur. Do as you please. It no longer concerns me. Baptiste, take Mister Holmes to my daughter's boudoir."

With that, the Marquis rose and left. Holmes watched him leave with astonishment, thinking "they are all the same; instead of watching over their children, they leave them to their own devices, and when a misfortune occurs, as it often will, they disown them…"

With these thoughts mulling through his head, the detective allowed himself to be guided through a maze of sumptuous rooms to a room hung in blue satin.

"This is the boudoir of the Comtesse," said Baptiste, the butler.

Holmes made a thorough but unproductive search of the room.

"Will you please ask the chambermaid to come," he said in frustration.

Baptiste left and returned, saying, "Dolly doesn't want to come, Monsieur."

"Bring her!"

The butler soon returned, literally carrying a struggling young woman in his arms. The girl wept and protested.

"Confess to Mister Holmes, Dolly. This is all your fault."

Dolly shook her head stubbornly.

"She's a famous piece and very clever," muttered the butler.

"Tell me, Dolly," said the detective, "did you help your mistress leave here, tonight, secretly?"

Silence. Dolly cast guilty but defiant looks at Baptiste and Holmes.

"It's too late to lie," added Holmes. "Something very bad has happened to the Comtesse."

This was too much for Dolly. Her resistance began to crumble.

"Yes," she confessed. "I often warned her, but she wouldn't listen to me. What could I do? I'm only her servant and I had to obey her."

"You should have informed her father."

Another silence. Dolly seemed to regret her weakness in speaking and relapsed into a determined resistance.

"Where did the Countess go when she left?"

More silence.

"Where?" said Holmes in a tone of command that Dolly could not resist.

"To see her lover, I suppose," she replied.

"Where was that?"

"I… I don't know," she muttered.

"Come on! You know perfectly!"

"No. I couldn't ask the Countess!"

Baptiste, itching to strangle Dolly, intervened.

"She's a liar, Mr. Holmes. Don't believe her. See this hand, Dolly? Would you like to know what it can do?"

Dolly cowered away from Baptiste.

"Make him go away, Mr. Holmes. I will tell you everything."

"Leave me alone with her," said Holmes to the butler.

"Since you insist, I'll go. But the little slut is clever. Watch out for her."

As Baptiste left, Dolly stuck out her tongue at him, then turned to Holmes ready to tell the truth to him, but not to Baptiste.

"I'll begin by warning you that I can cause very bad things to happen to you if I report you to the police," warned the detective.

"I'm going to tell you everything, Mr. Holmes. Six or eight months ago, the Comtesse was as beautiful and pure as an angel. But then, her father hired an American to give her riding lessons."

"Ah, it's always the same old story: the riding instructors, the music teachers, the dance masters that cause ravages in the best families. So they became lovers?"

Dolly nodded, weeping.

"What was the instructor's name?" asked Holmes.

"Charles Lake. He's a handsome young man. On a horse, he's like a god. They were always together."

"Where did they have private meetings?"

"In an opium den. I think the name of the proprietress was Madame Cajana. She rented them a room there under the pretext of smoking opium. In reality, it was a safe place for my mistress to see her lover."

"Excellent. One last thing: I'm certain you must have delivered many messages from your mistress to Mr. Lake. Where can I find him?"

"He lives not too far from here. I'll take you there if you like?"

"Yes, please."

"Give me time to put on a cloak."

A few minutes later, the Marquis de Malmaison, weeping at his window, watched Holmes and Dolly leave. He had given up trying to persuade himself that Jack the Ripper's latest victim was not his daughter. Alone, he could now give way to his despair.

## *VI . A Word Too Many*

"Be so good as to wake up, sir. I am Sherlock Holmes, the detective, and I must speak to you about a very serious matter."

"Huh?" said the sleeping figure of Charles Lake, at first unresponsive, but then reaching for his revolver on his night table.

Holmes quickly pushed the gun away.

"Didn't you hear me? I'm not a thief. I'm Sherlock Holmes!"

"Huh, what's it all about?" replied Lake.

"Get up and get dressed. The Comtesse de Malmaison has been murdered."

Lake, suddenly galvanized, leaped out of bed.

"Are you mad?"

"The Comtesse was murdered tonight in the opium den of Madame Cajana's—where she was in the habit of meeting you."

Lake wrapped himself in a red bath robe folded over a chair, clutching it tightly, with trembling hands.

"I can't grasp what you've just told me. In the opium den…?"

"Yes—of Madame Cajana. You yourself picked the spot."

"Suppose that were true? What do you want with me? Why have you come to bother me?"

"Take another tone or I'll have you arrested," said the detective. "On the spot."

"I had nothing to do with it. I know nothing about this crime," protested the American.

"But you had a rendezvous with her tonight?"

"We had agreed to meet tonight, it's true."

"At what time?"

"Ten. But I was late and when I got there..."

The American stopped.

"Well?" encouraged Holmes.

"I didn't find the ladder. The rope ladder that she would let down from the window."

"So you went home angry that she hadn't come to the rendezvous?"

"You seem to know everything."

"Well, I will tell you what happened. Someone knew your secret. He took your place and murdered her..."

The American burst into tears. Holmes scrutinized his face. His sorrow seemed to be genuine.

"If you really loved the Comtesse," said the Detective, now is the time to tell me as much as you can so I can catch her murderer."

"I ask nothing better," replied Charles Lake. "I did love her, but I knew we could never marry... Poor Irene! What a terrible end... I don't understand. Was she the victim of a burglar?"

"I don't know yet," said Holmes. "Please answer my questions. Who knew that the Comtesse and you were lovers?"

"I never told anyone. Only her chamber maid Dolly knew that we met at the opium den, but I'm pretty certain she didn't know how I got in. No one knew!"

"There must have been someone," pressed Holmes.

"Hold on! Yes! You're right! One man knew. But he couldn't be the murderer."

"That's for me to decide," said Holmes. "I've got to know this man's name."

After a long silence, the American whispered:

"You're a man who knows how to keep secrets, aren't you, Mr. Holmes? Can I trust you to not sully my dearest Irene's memory?"

"If it's at all humanly possible, you can trust me to remain discreet," replied the Detective.

"Very well. Our love had… consequences."

"You mean the Countess became pregnant?"

"Yes. So I… I consulted a physician."

"A doctor?"

"Yes. But the Doctor of whom I am speaking is very well known in London. He doesn't handle cases of this sort."

"Indeed."

"However, I had the opportunity to render him a service some years ago in Calcutta."

"Ah. He was in Calcutta?"

"Yes. He had bet a huge sum on a horse I was riding. I managed to win the race. If he had lost the bet, he'd have lost his fortune."

"Hmm. Now that's strange. A doctor who is also an audacious gambler."

Lake shrugged.

"There are gamblers everywhere. And the doctor was a gambler—but only on horses oddly enough." There was a pause, then the American continued: "When Irene told me she was in trouble, I didn't know what to do. I learned by chance that my doctor was in London where he now enjoys an immense reputation. So I went to him."

"His name?"

"Robert Fitzgerald."

"Doctor Fitzgerald? He's very well known, indeed."

"Yes, he's been successful here. In India, he didn't have much at first, but then, he married the daughter of a rich merchant. Since then, he's been a very respected man. He's succeeded in several difficult operations and even treated members of the royal family."

"Yes, I recall. A master surgeon. And he's the man in whom you confided?"

"Yes. I went to see him. He promised to help me."

"And you revealed to him the secret of your rendezvous with the Comtesse?"

"Yes. It was necessary. He said he couldn't do anything without examining the patient. But where? Irene wouldn't agree to see him at his surgery. So, in the end…"

"In the end, you decided to let him take your place?" asked Holmes. "Is that the truth?"

"Yes," admitted the American in a whisper.

"So you weren't late by accident."

Charles Lake remained silent.

"Listen to me, Mr. Lake," said the Detective. "I will do what I can for you. But what I did not tell you was that your lover was murdered by Jack the Ripper. And it would appear that Doctor Fitzgerald is indeed the Ripper himself."

Holmes bowed and left.

## *VII. A Mismatched Union*

It was nightfall near the statue of Lord Byron in Hyde Park. Captain Harry Thomson, a young English officer with blonde mustaches ,was waiting impatiently for someone. He began to pace up and down hitting flowers with his cane. Eventually, a young woman approached him.

"I was afraid you wouldn't come," he whispered.

"I almost wasn't able," she replied. "Robert didn't want to go out today to visit his patients as he usually does. Once he finally decided to go, I came as soon as I could."

The officer kissed her hand, then attempted to kiss her on the lips.

"You cannot kiss me here, Harry darling, someone might see us."

"We've got to put an end to this, Ruth! Let them see us. Don't I have the right?"

"I'm his legitimate wife."

"He stole you from me. Your father forced you to marry him!"

"You know it's you alone that I love."

"Are you happy with this man? You cannot be."

"He's my lawful spouse." Burning tears ran down the young woman's cheeks. There was a long silence. Then, she said: "Someone else might be happy with him. Sometimes he throws himself at my feet and adores me—like a divinity. But, there are days when he shuts himself up in his room without saying a word. Then, I think he's... insane."

"Insane? A doctor? How could he be?"

"He was bitten by a cobra in India. He recovered, but he changed. I think some of the snake's venom remained in his blood and drove him mad. Please, Harry, never tell another living soul what I've just told you!"

"Is that all?" asked the young Captain.

"He leaves the house at night, secretly. I know for certain. But where can he go? When he returns from these nocturnal expeditions, he shuts himself in his room immediately—and sleeps until noon..."

"Still, there's nothing so unusual in a doctor visiting his patient—at no matter what hour."

"That was my own explanation. And I thought nothing more about it; but recently, I found traces of blood on his bed and his pillow."

"Perhaps he'd performed an operation?"

"In the middle of the night?"

"In an urgent case."

There was another silence.

"About two weeks ago," Ruth continued, "I decided to stay on watch. I slept in a room adjoining that of my husband. I wanted to see if he'd actually returned. I watched through the keyhole. He returned, but dressed as a thief. His mustache was all awry."

"Are you sure it was him?"

"Of course, I'm sure."

"Why would he be in disguise?"

"I don't know. But it was my husband. I'm sure of it."

"The famous Doctor Fitzgerald prowling around London like an ordinary criminal... I can't believe it!"

“The next day,” said Ruth, “I asked the housekeeper if she’d seen my husband go out the night before. That’s when I learned that he never used the front door at night, but rather a backdoor leading in and out of our garden and into an alley behind our house; he’s the only one with the key. I also inspected his room and found a secret cabinet with the same disguises I’d seen him wear that night.”

Captain Thomson still looked incredulous.

“Could it be that he is secretly attending a patient from the East End, a beggar or a sailor, and it’s him whom you saw?”

Ruth shrugged his shoulders, realizing that no one would believe her.

“I can only say what I know,” she said with resignation. “I’m afraid of him.”

“Well then, the answer is simple: come live with me.”

“With you, Harry? But you know it’s impossible. I’d be a social outcast.”

“Would you like to stay with my mother, at least, until your father comes back from India? You know how much she adores you.”

“I can’t. Robert is insanely jealous. He barely lets me out of the house as it is me. If he found out I’m still seeing you… Oh, how much he hates you. I can’t imagine what he might do! But tomorrow, he has to attend a medical conference. He won’t be back until long after midnight. We can…”

Harry hugged Ruth again, despite her protests, and pressed burning kisses to her lips.

The two lovers stood up and left arm in arm. Shortly after they were out of sight, Sherlock Holmes emerged from the shrubbery where he had been listening with great attention.

"When one wants to penetrate a man's secrets, one must follow his wife. Good idea I had to follow her for the last several days. Now, for the husband!"

## *VIII. A Complacent Gentleman*

"It's your turn now," said the orderly to a plump, elderly gentleman, who had been sitting in Doctor Fitzgerald's waiting room most of the afternoon. "You're our last patient of the day. Sorry for the long wait."

"It's quite all right," said the gentleman, using his cane to stand up. "When one chooses to consult a physician as well-known as Doctor Fitzgerald, one must be prepared to wait a little."

The orderly introduced the elderly patient into the doctor's surgery, then closed the padded leather door behind him.

Doctor Fitzgerald was sitting behind his desk and did not raise his head, not look at the patient, as the elderly gentleman approached.

"Excuse me, doctor?" said the man, with a little cough.

Doctor Fitzgerald pulled out of his reverie; his face was pale and his features drawn. There were circles under his piercing, dark eyes. He looked at the elderly gentleman standing before him with an expression of surprise.

"I thought I'd seen my last patient for the day. Who are you, sir?"

"I'm not a patient, doctor," said the gentleman.

"You say you have no complaint, sir?"

"That's correct. I didn't come to see you as a patient, Doctor Fitzgerald."

"In that case, be brief," replied the doctor brusquely. "I am here only for those who are ill."

"Oh, doctor, it's no concern of mine, but—ah, how bad women are. Yes. Bad, very bad... So bad that they ought to be made to vanish from the surface of the Earth and return to Hell from whence they came. Like serpents. At least, one can crush serpents. Serpents have been the preferred companions of the Daughters of Eve. Read the Bible. Yes. It was the serpent that got us expelled from Paradise…"

"What are you talking about?" said the doctor, increasingly annoyed by the man's ramblings.

"I'm talking about Captain Harry Thomson."

Doctor Fitzgerald reacted as if he had been struck by lightning. His lips trembled; his eyes became wide as saucers.

"Who are you?" he said finally. "How do you know that name? What does this all mean?"

"My name's Jack Connor. I manufacture soap. I no longer need to work so I stroll around…"

"Come to the point!"

"Yesterday, at dusk, I was near the Byron statue in Hyde Park. I fell asleep on a bench. Hearing voices, I soon woke up. It was obvious the people talking were lovers."

"Lovers?" repeated the doctor, trembling.

"Kissing, hugging… I couldn't get up and leave without embarrassing them—and, more importantly, myself. And I couldn't avoid hearing the conversation. The young woman had given the officer, whose name was Harry Thomson, a secret rendezvous. She was complaining about her husband—who, it seems, according to her…"

"Well?"

"…Makes nocturnal excursions in disguise."

"Really? She said that?"

"And she named her husband..."

"Shut up!"

"It was one Doctor Fitzgerald. A famous and respected surgeon. Then, they kissed and made another rendezvous."

"Shut up! I don't want to hear another word." But then, the doctor hesitated and changed his mind. "Hold on, yes, speak. I want to know. I want to know everything."

"But I have nothing more to tell you," said the gentleman, "except that they will meet while you attend a medical society conference this evening. At Walworth Street. Adieu, doctor."

And the disguised Sherlock Holmes bowed and left. Doctor Fitzgerald stared after him thoughtfully.

"Aren't you going to the Medical Society meeting, Robert?," asked Ruth Fitzgerald. "You'll be late."

Robert Fitzgerald sat staring into space, a vacant look on his face. Finally, he answered his wife:

"Yes, it's true. Would you like to go with me?"

"But only men attend."

"I could get you in the balcony. You could look around. You could find a man—men—to your taste."

"What a thing to say to me. In fact, it's unsupportable. You always contrive to make my life unbearable. I think we'd best separate."

"You really think it would be better for us to separate? Where would you go?"

"I'll manage."

"No doubt—with your lover!"

He grabbed her, seizing her by the wrists and forcing her to kneel.

"Let me go or I will call for help," said Ruth. She managed to wiggle loose and added: "If you hurt me, I have a friend who will demand an account from you."

That last remark was more than the doctor could stand. With an inhuman roar, he lunged again and grabbed his wife by the neck. His eyes were manic and full of murderous rage. A light, rosy froth escaped from his lips.

"Die! die! Bitch! Ah, the sluts! Let them all die. Race of vipers! I am appointed by the Lord God! The Lord appeared to me and said: Kill, kill the serpents!" he screamed as he tried to strangle her.

Ruth thought her last hour had come, but suddenly her husband stopped and released her.

"Go away, I beg you. I was out of my mind. But you provoked me. I know I love you. Madly. I only want your happiness. I know you've been faithful to me. Do you still love me?"

"You are my husband," she said clutching at her neck, with only one desire: to flee. "I must love you. I will be faithful. But there must be no more scenes like this between us."

"No. There won't be," said the doctor, all his energies seemingly spent. "Leave me alone now. I've got to dress for the meeting."

She offered him her cheek to kiss and rushed out of the house.

After Ruth had left, the doctor locked the door, took out his medical bag and administered an injection of morphine to himself.

## *IX. Sherlock Holmes Wins His Bet*

"Holmes, your disguise surpasses anything of the sort I've seen you do before," said Watson to the seemingly tall, elegantly dressed woman who stood near the barely lit entrance of a house in Walworth Street. "You look just like a streetwalker!"

"Thank you, Watson. But I hear a cab… It must be Mrs. Fitzgerald. Go tell her what I told you. I'll wait here."

The cab stopped a couple of houses down the street and Ruth stepped onto the sidewalk. Suddenly, Watson was at her side, grabbing her arm.

"Quickly, Madame, come with me!"

"Who are you, sir?"

"My name is Doctor Watson. I'm here on behalf of Sherlock Holmes."

"The famous detective?"

"Yes. But come. There's no time to lose. Your husband is following you."

"My husband!" blurted out the terrified woman.

"A terrible fate awaits you if you do not come. He's been told everything."

"Great god. Then my husband knows…"

"Everything, Madame. He knows that you plan to see Captain Harry Thompson this very night while he attends the medical society meeting. He may appear at any moment. Will you trust me?"

Ruth nodded weakly and the two disappeared in an adjacent street.

Meanwhile, Holmes, still dressed as a woman, waited in Walworth Street for Doctor Fitzgerald to appear.

Soon, he spotted him, disguised as a tramp. The Detective couldn't help but feel a certain apprehension. The next few minutes would seal the fate of Jack the Ripper!

Holmes sauntered up to him and in a Cockney voice said: "Where are you going, sweetie? I think it would nice for us to be alone together—just the two of us, tonight? Only a shilling."

Doctor Fitzgerald placed his arm about her.

"Just the two of us. You—and Jack the Ripper!"

Fitzgerald pulled out his knife and tried to stab his intended victim, but Holmes was wearing body armor concealed by the female dress, and the murderous blow was harmlessly deflected.

A terrible battle ensued. Finally, Holmes knocked out Fitzgerald and dragged him to the waiting cab.

"To Scotland Yard! Don't spare the horses!"

"You are certain of this, Lestrade?" said Superintendant Warren.

"Grover Bell has confessed to murdering his sister in hopes of inheriting her fortune," proclaimed Inspector Lestrade proudly.

"And you think he's Jack The Ripper?"

"Yes, Mr. Warren, I'm sure of it."

"Has he confessed to being the Ripper?"

"Not yet. But he will."

"Perhaps," said Holmes, entering, still dressed as a harlot, but rather the worse for wear from the struggle with Doctor Fitzgerald. "But whether he does or not, Grover Bell is not Jack the Ripper, this man is."

Two Police Officers entered with Doctor Fitzgerald supported between them.

Fitzgerald was incoherent, literally frothing at the mouth. Holmes pulled off his false beard revealing his true identity to the surprised Lestrade and Warren. Explanations followed.

"I must congratulate you, Lestrade," said Holmes. "Grover Bell did murder his sister and you were correct in arresting him. But he only imitated the Ripper—and not very cleverly. He saw an opportunity to blame the crime on the Ripper and acted accordingly. But he wasn't the real Ripper. Doctor Fitzgerald was."

Doctor Fitzgerald vanished into a mental institution where, in a moment of lucidity, he managed to kill himself. His wife is now happily married to Captain Thompson, and Sherlock Holmes remains THE KING OF DETECTIVES.

## SF & FANTASY

Henri Allorge. *The Great Cataclysm*
Guy d'Armen. *Doc Ardan: The City of Gold and Lepers*
G.-J. Arnaud. *The Ice Company*
Cyprien Bérard. *The Vampire Lord Ruthwen*
Aloysius Bertrand. *Gaspard de la Nuit*
Richard Bessière. *The Gardens of the Apocalypse*
Albert Bleunard. *Ever Smaller*
Félix Bodin. *The Novel of the Future*
Alphonse Brown. *City of Glass*
André Caroff. *The Terror of Madame Atomos; Miss Atomos; The Return of Madame Atomos*
Félicien Champsaur. *The Human Arrow*
Didier de Chousy. *Ignis*
Captain Danrit. *Undersea Odyssey*
C. I. Defontenay. *Star (Psi Cassiopeia)*
Charles Derennes. *The People of the Pole*
Georges Dodds (anthologist). *The Missing Link*
Harry Dickson. *The Heir of Dracula*
Jules Dornay. *Lord Ruthven Begins*
Sâr Dubnotal *vs. Jack the Ripper*
Alexandre Dumas. *The Return of Lord Ruthven*
Renée Dunan. *Baal*
J.-C. Dunyach. *The Night Orchid; The Thieves of Silence*
Henri Duvernois. *The Man Who Found Himself*
Achille Eyraud. *Voyage to Venus*
Henri Falk. *The Age of Lead*
Paul Féval. *Anne of the Isles; Knightshade; Revenants; Vampire City; The Vampire Countess; The Wandering Jew's Daughter*
Paul Féval, *fils. Felifax, the Tiger-Man*
Charles de Fieux. *Lamékis*
Arnould Galopin. *Doctor Omega*; *Doctor Omega & The Shadowmen*
G.L. Gick. *Harry Dickson and the Werewolf of Rutherford Grange*
Nathalie Henneberg. *The Green Gods*
V. Hugo, P. Foucher & P. Meurice. *The Hunchback of Notre-Dame*
Michel Jeury. *Chronolysis*
Octave Joncquel & Theo Varlet. *The Martian Epic*
Gérard Klein. *The Mote in Time's Eye*
Jean de La Hire. *Enter the Nyctalope; The Nyctalope on Mars; The Nyctalope vs. Lucifer*
Etienne-Léon de Lamothe-Langon. *The Virgin Vampire*

André Laurie. *Spiridon*
Gabriel de Lautrec. *The Vengeance of the Oval Portrait*
Georges Le Faure & Henri de Graffigny. *The Extraordinary Adventures of a Russian Scientist Across the Solar System* (2 vols.)
Gustave Le Rouge. *The Vampires of Mars*
Jules Lermina. *Mysteryville; Panic in Paris; To-Ho and the Gold Destroyers; The Secret of Zippelius*
Jean-Marc & Randy Lofficier. *Edgar Allan Poe on Mars; The Katrina Protocol; Pacifica; Robonocchio; Tales of the Shadowmen 1-7*
Xavier Mauméjean. *The League of Heroes*
José Moselli. *Illa's End*
John-Antoine Nau. *Enemy Force*
Marie Nizet. *Captain Vampire*
C. Nodier, A. Beraud & Toussaint-Merle. *Frankenstein*
Henri de Parville. *An Inhabitant of the Planet Mars*
J. Polidori, C. Nodier, E. Scribe. *Lord Ruthven the Vampire*
P.-A. Ponson du Terrail. *The Vampire and the Devil's Son*
Maurice Renard. *The Blue Peril; Doctor Lerne; The Doctored Man; A Man Among the Microbes; The Master of Light*
Albert Robida. *The Adventures of Saturnin Farandoul; The Clock of the Centuries; Chalet in the Sky*
J.-H. Rosny Aîné. *Helgvor of the Blue River; The Givreuse Enigma; The Mysterious Force; The Navigators of Space; Vamireh; The World of the Variants; The Young Vampire*
Marcel Rouff. *Journey to the Inverted World*
Han Ryner. *The Superhumans*
Brian Stableford. *The New Faust at the Tragicomique;The Empire of the Necromancers (The Shadow of Frankenstein; Frankenstein and the Vampire Countess; Frankenstein in London); Sherlock Holmes & The Vampires of Eternity; The Stones of Camelot; The Wayward Muse.* (anthologist) *The Germans on Venus; News from the Moon; The Supreme Progress; The World Above the World*
Jacques Spitz. *The Eye of Purgatory*
Kurt Steiner. *Ortog*
Eugène Thébault. *Radio-Terror*
C.-F. Tiphaigne de La Roche. *Amilec*
Paul Vibert. *The Mysterious Fluid*
Villiers de l'Isle-Adam. *The Scaffold; The Vampire Soul*
Philippe Ward. *Artahe*
Philippe Ward & Sylvie Miller. *The Song of Montségur*

## MYSTERIES & THRILLERS

M. Allain & P. Souvestre. *The Daughter of Fantômas*
A. Anicet-Bourgeois, Lucien Dabril. *Rocambole*
A. Bisson & G. Livet. *Nick Carter vs. Fantômas*
V. Darlay & H. de Gorsse. *Lupin vs. Holmes: The Stage Play*
Paul Féval. *Gentlemen of the Night; John Devil; The Black Coats ('Salem Street; The Invisible Weapon; The Parisian Jungle; The Companions of the Treasure; Heart of Steel; The Cadet Gang; The Sword-Swallower)*
Emile Gaboriau. *Monsieur Lecoq*
Steve Leadley. *Sherlock Holmes: The Circle of Blood*
Maurice Leblanc. *Arsène Lupin vs. Countess Cagliostro; Lupin vs. Holmes (The Blonde Phantom; The Hollow Needle)*
Gaston Leroux. *Chéri-Bibi; The Phantom of the Opera; Rouletabille & the Mystery of the Yellow Room*
William Patrick Maynard. *The Terror of Fu Manchu*
Frank J. Morlock. *Sherlock Holmes: The Grand Horizontals; Sherlock Holmes vs Jack the Ripper*
P. de Wattyne & Y. Walter. *Sherlock Holmes vs. Fantômas*
David White. *Fantômas in America*

## SCREENPLAYS

Mike Baron. *The Iron Triangle*
Emma Bull & Will Shetterly. *Nightspeeder; War for the Oaks*
Gerry Conway & Roy Thomas. *Doc Dynamo*
Steve Englehart. *Majorca*
James Hudnall. *The Devastator*
Jean-Marc & Randy Lofficier. *Royal Flush*
J.-M. & R. Lofficier & Marc Agapit. *Despair*
Andrew Paquette. *Peripheral Vision*
R. Thomas, J. Hendler & L. Sprague de Camp. *Rivers of Time*

## NON-FICTION

Stephen R. Bissette. *Blur 1-5; Green Mountain Cinema 1; Teen Angels & New Mutants*
Win Scott Eckert. *Crossovers* (2 vols.)
Jean-Marc & Randy Lofficier. *Shadowmen* (2 vols.)
Randy Lofficier. *Over Here*

CPSIA information can be obtained at www.ICGtesting.com
Printed in the USA
LVOW081626140212
268675LV00001B/57/P